"What does interest you, Miss Allen?"

The duke spoke sincerely, though Amelia was vexed to see that he was thoroughly amused.

"A tour of the Continent," he suggested. "Perhaps a visit to the Paris salons?"

He talked smoothly on, mentioning other pleasurable pastimes, and Amelia's fury mounted.

"It is surely within my power to provide *some* pleasure that would excite your interest," he concluded.

"I fear not, Your Grace," she said, affecting a yawn. "It has been my experience that no pastime can be truly diverting if shared with a dull companion." Amelia rose, determined to leave.

The duke also rose, still smiling complacently. "I assure you, Miss Allen, my company would be anything but dull."

"That's as may be, Your Grace," she said sweetly. "But I would sooner spend a day in Bedlam than one more minute in your exalted company!"

Books by Eva Rutland

HARLEQUIN REGENCY ROMANCE

1–MATCHED PAIR
20–THE VICAR'S DAUGHTER
28–ENTERPRISING LADY

HARLEQUIN ROMANCE

2897–TO LOVE THEM ALL
2944–AT FIRST SIGHT
3064–NO ACCOUNTING FOR LOVE

Don't miss any of our special offers. Write to us at the following address for information on our newest releases.

Harlequin Reader Service
P.O. Box 1397, Buffalo, NY 14240
Canadian address: P.O. Box 603,
Fort Erie, Ont. L2A 5X3

THE WILLFUL LADY

EVA RUTLAND

Harlequin Books

TORONTO • NEW YORK • LONDON
AMSTERDAM • PARIS • SYDNEY • HAMBURG
STOCKHOLM • ATHENS • TOKYO • MILAN

Published March 1991

ISBN 0-373-31145-1

THE WILLFUL LADY

CHAPTER ONE

IN THE MIDST of the cotillion, Amelia Allen stumbled. She quickly regained her step and danced with her usual grace, but her eyes continued to stray to one corner of the ballroom where Jewel, her stepmother, was flirting outrageously with the elegant gentleman who had created such a stir when he came in. "A duke," someone had whispered to Amelia. Not that it signified to Jewel. She would ply her wiles on any man who gave her the slightest attention, and there were many who did.

"I'm glad you came." Lord Conway, her partner said as the figures of the dance brought them together once more. "I was afraid you wouldn't."

"Oh, how could you think so? Surely you must know that I would not have missed your sister's engagement party." And she would not have. Connie Stewart had been her very best friend since that first day at Madame Suffield's Academy. Amelia had been privy to all the trysts and spats leading to this betrothal and had a vested interest in the outcome. She would not have disappointed Connie for all the world.

But Jewel... She darted another quick glance at that lady. Shocking! Thank goodness that Papa, too fatigued to dance, had retired to the card room and was not a witness to his wife's perfidy.

Poor Papa. Amelia was worried about his frequent bouts of fatigue. He had not yet finished the portrait of Lady Fitzgerald, and she was becoming impatient. Amelia pondered an idea that she had been toying with since her return home. Could she—or would Papa let her—finish the portrait for him? Of course she did not presume to possess her father's talent, but if she took great care...

"Would you like champagne, or perhaps a glass of punch?" asked Lord Conway as he led her from the dance floor.

"Punch would be nice, thank you."

He procured the refreshment, and she sipped it gratefully. "So refreshing," she told him, as over the rim of her glass she examined more closely the man with her stepmother. "Your mother's ball is a delight. I am enjoying myself immensely," she said, but her mind was elsewhere. Was this the man she had seen riding with Jewel in the Park a few days ago? And perhaps it was more than a flirtation. Mayhap Jewel had another destination in mind when she conjured up so many shopping expeditions and teas. Amelia was not as blind as her father to his wife's peccadilloes.

"And when do you plan to return to Oxford?" Amelia asked Lord Conway, striving to keep her voice calm and disguise her disgust. Jewel was now contriving to whisper something of an intimate nature in her companion's ear by spreading her fan to hide her face. It was at that moment that Amelia heard the scraping of chairs in the card room next door. Heavens! Her father would be returning and would see.

"Please excuse me," she said quickly. "I must speak to my mama." Mama. Wouldn't that throw Jewel into a rage, Amelia thought as she hurried across to join the couple. Could she lure the gentleman away from Jewel? In any event, if she were to join the two of them, her father might not think anything was untoward.

Her only wish was to save her papa from hurt and her only fault was that she moved too rapidly. Or perhaps it was Jewel who erred when she snapped her fan shut and startled an approaching waiter. The waiter started, bumped into Amelia and lost control of his tray. The ensuing crash of glasses and Jewel's screech claimed the attention of everyone in the room.

"Oh, you clumsy oaf! See what you have done!" Jewel's lovely face momentarily contorted into a scowl as she shook drops of champagne from her dress. Then, remembering where she was, she smiled sweetly at her audience before rushing away to repair the damage.

Amelia was aghast. Not that she cared a whit that Jewel's glamorous gown was probably ruined. She was more concerned about the frightened waiter who bent to retrieve the broken bits of glass.

"It's not his fault," Amelia said to the few people who had gathered round, and to her hostess, who came forward. "Oh, Lady Stewart, my apologies. I fear it was entirely my doing. I was in such a rush to speak with my...to Jewel. I am sorry."

Lady Stewart was all that was kind. Another waiter was summoned to help, and within moments order and conviviality were restored. She had not meant to cause such a disturbance, but at least her purpose had been served, Amelia thought as she turned away in relief.

"One moment, if you please." The words and tone were polite enough, but there was something formidable in the stance of the tall man who blocked her path. She could not mistake the mockery masked by the smile he affected in his fine dark eyes. "Surely you are not going to desert me now."

"Desert you?"

"Not after all the trouble you took to secure my attention. Now that you have succeeded in detaching me from my lovely companion—"

"Oh . . . !" She bit back the words 'conceited coxcomb,' but she could not stem the flood of anger. He would not have dared speak thus to any lady in the room except the daughter of Victor Allen. Well, if his tongue could be so unguarded, then so could hers! "Oh, my dear sir, I do forgive you," she said softly.

"Forgive me. For what, pray tell?"

"For having the unmitigated gall to imply that I would resort to such tactics or indeed for the egotistical assumption that I wished to secure your company. But of course I realize that such conjecture is only natural," she said, changing her tone and smiling sweetly. "For your exalted station must often make you the prey of designing females. However, I hasten to assure your grace that I am extremely discriminating in my tastes and you have nothing to fear from me.

Good evening, sir." Her taffeta skirt rustled stiffly as she swept round him and went to join her father. She only wished she could have been more insulting.

But he was more amused than insulted, though perhaps a bit chagrined, for her verbal arrows had been a palpable hit. Guy Courtland Grosvenor, Marquis of Brookhaven, Earl of Tappen, and Ninth Duke of Winston, was certainly often the object of avaricious females but was rarely the object of a stinging set down. He stared at the neat, retreating figure of the vixen who had brought him to book. So she had a temper and a tongue to match that fiery red hair! And had taken him to task for assuming that she had desired his interest. Gad! What else could he have thought? He was aware that she had been watching him for the past half hour, and with such speculation in those flashing green eyes. Oh, what else was he to assume? But just who *was* she?

"She's a nobody! Pray, do not stare in that manner." His mother clutched his sleeve. "And at such a one. Just the kind of lightskirt whom you must stay clear of. I can't imagine what possessed Emma Stewart to invite them. Now, dear, come with me. I want you to meet Lord Worthington's daughter, Elise." She led him off to meet yet another lady worthy to become the future Duchess of Winston.

His determined mother kept him so occupied with estimable ladies of the ton that he had no opportunity to enquire about the intriguing redhead with the flashing green eyes. No matter. The Season was in full swing, and doubtless he would encounter her at Almack's or at some other boring affair.

As Amelia entered the Allen carriage, she felt she had acquitted herself well.

At least, she had celebrated Connie's betrothal and was thankful that this would be the only Society affair they would have to attend, and indeed, the only one they would have been invited to. The behaviour that passed for gracious hospitality in the house over which Jewel presided appeared crass and scandalous to the ton. Possibly, she mused, they were not aware that no behaviour seemed outlandish at Victor Allen's home.

Good heaven! Had her long sojourn at Madame Suffield's Academy given her airs? She was becoming as vulgarly disdainful of her father's bohemian household as the rest of London! A guilty flush stained her cheeks. But she was jolted out of her reverie as their carriage swerved to allow a smart curricle to speed by.

She sat up straighter. She couldn't be sure in the dark, but she was almost certain it was the same vehicle she had seen Jewel riding in. The same man with whom Jewel had flirted this night. She glanced at her stepmother to see if she had noticed. But Jewel's whole attention was now centred on her husband.

"Victor, darling," she crooned, reaching up to stroke his chin. "I am persuaded that you did enjoy yourself, didn't you? I vow that it is good for you to get away from that stuffy old studio. Here," she said, placing a rug over his knees. "The night is a little chilly."

Amelia could not see her father's face but she knew he was smiling and imagined that the fatigued expression he so often wore was less in evidence. It was always thus when Jewel fussed over him. And indeed she was always doing so. She made him very happy and it was unkind to think such dreadful things about her. With such beauty Jewel could not be blamed for the fact that so many men were attracted to her.

It was very possible, Amelia thought as the carriage rumbled through the cobblestone streets, that her suspicions were unwarranted. After all, they had been happily married for four years and she had only been with them for four months. And, yes, she had been against this marriage from the start; she had been bitter that her father had found a replacement for her own mother, the lovely, vivacious Venetia, and so soon after her death.

"It has only been one year." Amelia, sixteen at the time, had sobbed in the arms of kind Madame Suffield.

"Have you thought how that year has been for him?" asked the wise woman, "without your mother and without you? In spite of how much he must have wanted you to return home, he has adhered to the promise made to your mother that you would remain here to finish your instruction. She wanted you to have all the attributes of a perfect lady."

Her words brought fresh tears, for it conjured up a vision of Venetia as she uttered her constant admonition to her daughter: "Always be a lady, but never marry a gentleman." She would laugh as she tossed back her red hair and her green eyes twinkled as she added, "Marry a *gentle man* instead, like your papa, who has made me the happiest woman alive."

Venetia had been a gentleman's daughter who had broken her engagement to the noble Duke of Reed and run off to Gretna Green with the impoverished artist who had been hired to do her betrothal portrait, Victor Allen. Her enraged father had disinherited her and broken off all communication with her. But Venetia had never regretted it for one moment. "It takes more than rank and money to make a happy marriage," she often declared.

After Victor's marriage to Jewel, Amelia did not wish to return home. She had remained at Madame Suffield's after her classmates left to make their entry into Society. For the past two years she had been teaching the art classes and would still be doing so had she not received an urgent message from Mrs. Stokes, her father's housekeeper: "Come home, Amelia. Your father needs you."

And indeed he does need me Amelia thought as the carriage drew to a stop before their residence in Fitzroy Square. Though the hour was late, she saw with irritation that the large front parlour was ablaze with light. She wondered how many callers would have to be dismissed. Associates of Victor Allen, for they could not all be called friends, had got into the habit of treating his home rather like their private club. They would gather there each evening to read aloud their poems or their latest treatises on the state of the nation, to perform a new musical composition or exhibit a painting, or perhaps merely to sit and have a comfortable coze and sip Victor Allen's wine. They always felt welcome, even in the absence of the host, for it was a cosy comfortable place where a man felt at ease, even if accompanied by his mistress.

Victor, Jewel and Amelia entered the house to the sound of a high-pitched soprano voice delivering a rollicking song. The tinkling notes of the pianoforte reverberated to the bawdy accompanying refrain.

"Ah! That's Rita. Practicing for her audition tomorrow." Victor, always the congenial host and indulgent critic, turned towards the parlour. "Let's go in and lend our encouragement."

"And tell them all about the grand ball at Stewart House." Jewel, her eyes alight with her success at rubbing elbows with the upper ten thousand, was about to follow when Amelia pulled both of them back. "You're tired, Papa. We mustn't let him overdo, Jewel, or he shall never attend another ball." Ignoring the obstinate glint in Jewel's eyes, she firmly maneouvered the couple to the stairs. "It's been a long night, Papa, and you know you have an early sitting with Lady Fitzgerald tomorrow."

Victor, too fatigued to resist, submitted and, followed by his reluctant wife, mounted the stairs. "But Rita needs a bit of bolstering," he advised his daughter. "You go in and applaud her efforts."

Rita LaCrosse, if indeed that was her real name, was an aspiring comic actress and the latest "temporary" occupant of one of the spare bedrooms in the Allen residence. Amelia would have been willing to do her utmost to ensure Rita's acceptance into any theatrical company that would take the girl on a long tour far from London. But at the moment Rita's ribald song and the laughter from her appreciative audience was echoing throughout the house. If Papa was to have any peace... Amelia braced herself and entered the parlour.

"It just ain't got the proper bounce, Rita," said the chubby balding man at the pianoforte. "Wait. When I start it here—*ta de dum da*—that's when you come out with— Oh, haloo, Amy, join us do," he said as if inviting Amelia into his own quarters. "Listen to Rita's latest and give us your say so."

"I've already heard it. And I think it's quite the thing, Rita."

"Oh, do you think so, dearie?" Rita turned her gamine face to Amelia, her blue eyes wide with that ludicrous expression of perpetual enquiry that had prompted Victor to suggest that she stick to comic rather than dramatic renditions. "Or do you think, like Tubby here, that it needs a bit more bounce?"

"No, I do not. I think it quite perfect as it is. And I think you should save your breath for tomorrow's audition. Really, Mr. Tubbs, you are demanding too much and straining poor Rita's voice, and I will not permit it," Amelia said as she firmly closed the lid of the pianoforte. "And truly, it is late. I think we could all do with some rest."

Only one of the several occupants in the room protested as Amelia began to snuff out candles.

An attractive and fashionably dressed young woman rose from the sofa and tugged at her companion's sleeve. "Come along, ducky. We're being given the shove. Downright inhospitable, I calls it."

"Dear me! I fear I am being shockingly uncivil," Amelia said as she pulled the bell rope for John, who had been waiting in the kitchen until called to escort the visitors out. She smiled sweetly at the woman and tried to ignore the stare she was receiving from the elegant gentleman who accompanied her.

"Nonsense, my dear," he said good-naturedly. "A woman with your obvious charm could never be uncivil." His hazel eyes travelled appreciatively over Amelia, making her extremely conscious of the bareness of her shoulders above her low-cut evening gown.

"Then I pray you'll forgive me for interrupting your evening's entertainment," she said, but did not waver until she had ushered all visitors out. She followed John into the hall to assure herself of Mr. Tubbs's departure, and seeing him smile wistfully after Rita as she mounted the stairs, suspected there had been occasions when he had crept up them with her. But never again. *I will not allow my father's house to become a brothel,* Amelia vowed as she returned to the parlour to rouse old Timothy, who still sat half dozing and half foxed.

Timothy, a wizened old man with a wooden leg, was Victor's other houseguest, and his status was more permanent than temporary. Still, Amelia reflected as she led the dazed man towards the stairs, he might yet become a paying guest. He was beginning to sell some of his scrimshaws, which were really quite good. No doubt he had had plenty of time to practice the art of carving designs on shells and whale bones during his long voyages on the high seas; possibly on a pirate ship, Amelia thought, judging by his predilection for rum and the vocabulary of the parrot which roosted on a pedestal in his room. She liked Timothy. He was always in good humour and he did try to pay his way by tidying Victor's studio and sharpening his pencils and cleaning his brushes.

Due to a lack of funds and therefore a lack of servants, Amelia's last chore was to help John take out the glasses and straighten the parlour. No matter what occurred in the evening, during the daylight hours Victor's residence must be respectable enough for fashionable ladies to climb to his top-floor studio to sit for their portraits.

THE NEXT MORNING Amelia rose early to set up the easel and lay out the paint pots for her father. When Lady Fitzgerald arrived, she had tea ready and helped to seat her. Victor disliked having an audience while he worked, so Amelia did not linger. But she had noticed the weariness in his face and saw his hand tremble when he picked up the brush. She studied Lady Fitzgerald's face, then went immediately to her room and sketched it from memory. Perhaps, if she had to, she could finish the portrait.

Afterwards she sought out Mrs. Stokes to ask if she could assist her by doing the shopping. She found her in Timothy's room.

"Indeed, I would be most grateful, Missy. Such a good child, just like your dear mother." Mrs. Stokes, only a slip of a girl at the time, had been Venetia's personal maid. She had gone with her mistress to Gretna Green and had remained in the Allen household, eventually becoming housekeeper. She still idolized Venetia and always referred to her successor as "that one." "My lady Venetia took hold of the crazy goings-on in this house, begging your pardon, Missy. But it's like your mama said: your papa's the best man alive, but people take advantage, and that's a fact! And it's a shame how it is now, I tell you. Everything topsy-turvy and that one still abed and ordering that her chocolate be sent up.

"Mercy save us, but I'm glad you're here," Mrs. Stokes continued as she emptied two bottles into a dustbin and began to remove the sheets from the bed. "And I'm that glad old Timothy's seen fit to go out. 'Bout time we gave this room a good cleaning. Smells like an ale house."

"Indeed it does," said Amelia, going over to throw open the casement. "Let's give it a good airing."

"Blimey, mate!" croaked the parrot who, until that moment, had been as quiet as you please. "Walk the plank, blast you!" With a great flap of wings he flew out of the window and into the park beyond the house.

"Oh, Sylvester!" Amelia wailed. "Come back!"

"Mercy save us!" screamed Mrs. Stokes. "Old Timothy will give us what for when he finds his parrot up and gone."

"He'll not find him gone," declared Amelia. "Let me have one of those sheets." She took it and ran quickly downstairs, grabbed a handful of biscuits and ran out into the park calling "Sylvester! Sylvester, come! I have a treat for you." But Sylvester was enjoying his freedom and paid her no heed. He flapped from tree to bush and to yet another tree as if he wished to display his red and green feathers from every angle.

It was not a fashionable park or a very well kept one, and Amelia tore her skirt, lost one shoe and got her hair tangled in bushes as she valiantly followed the colourful bird, still calling, "Please, Sylvester. Come! Biscuit!"

But Sylvester continued to swoop from tree to bush, pausing now and again to survey the sheet and blurt out such epithets as "Ahoy, skipper! Avast, mate!"

The chase lasted for perhaps half an hour before the parrot seemed to tire. He rested on a low branch and Amelia knelt on the riding path a few feet away, whispering, "Come, Sylvester. Here's a biscuit. Sweet biscuit." She knew he would approach eventually and then she would quickly throw the sheet over him. Any minute now...

The Duke of Winston hated the fashionable parks of London where well-born people converged in costly equipage to parade and nod and impede one another's progress. He preferred unfashionable parks, or an empty field if one could be found, where he could let his horse have its head, and where he could enjoy a wild romp with the wind whistling through his hair. It was a bright, sunny day and he galloped freely through the deserted, unkempt park, wishing there were hedges to sail over or streams to ford. Still, there were no impediments and—

What the devil! He tightened his hold on the reins as his horse bolted, startled by the loud screeching and the flash of red and green that whizzed past. Miraculously, he did manage to avoid trampling the girl who was kneeling directly in his path. As soon as he got Timber under control, he checked the horse and turned back to confront her, intending to give her a good scold.

Yet when he pulled up beside her, he perceived that this was a damsel in distress: her dress was torn, her red hair had tumbled to her waist and was entangled with twigs and leaves and she looked quite distraught. He dismounted and started to ask how he might help her.

But the face lifted to him was one of fury. She threw up her hands and stamped a stocking-clad foot hard on the ground. "Now look what you've done! You blundering paperskull!"

CHAPTER TWO

HE STARED AT THE GIRL. She was . . . No, she couldn't be. But . . . Yes, that red hair. That voice. Dishevelled though she was, he knew she could only be the little vixen from the evening before.

Though she had been dressed in the first stave of fashion then and looked little more than a street urchin now, he would know those flashing green eyes and sharp tongue anywhere.

"Let me remind you," he said, trying to keep his temper under control, "that this is a riding path, not a church. When you wish to kneel in prayer—"

"Be good enough to spare me your wit, sir! And you are quite right. This is a riding path, not a racing track! And for you to come thundering along in that reckless fashion, frightening Sylvester and . . . Oh, dear!" She made a frantic gesture and turned away, calling softly, "Sylvester!"

Sylvester? A child? He started to follow her. "Wait. I'll help you find him."

She turned back. "I don't need your help. I was doing very well by myself until you came along. Will you just go! Take your horse and—"

"Walk the plank! Scurvy dog!"

Winston jumped, unnerved by the loud squawking which came from the air somewhere above his shoulder.

"What the devil!" he exclaimed as he tried to steady his horse.

"Oh, shut up, you idiotish strutting peacock! I've a mind to leave you here to be caught by some wild beast!" Then suddenly the girl's voice softened to pleading. "Here's a biscuit. Sweet biscuit. Come, Sylvester."

Winston followed her gaze to see a parrot perched on the limb of a tree across the path. The bird observed them solemnly, but Winston received the strange impression that the blasted bird was grinning.

So that was it! She was trying to catch her pet. Well, if he moved carefully and quickly... But the bird was quicker. He swooped away just as Winston lunged, his screeching rending the air. "Shiver me timbers. Ha, matey!"

"Oh, good heavens, you've frightened him off again. Please, sir, leave us be. Take your horse and go away."

"But I was only trying to help. If you wish to catch your parrot—"

"He is *not* my parrot and I do not especially wish to catch him. Only," she added, sounding quite tired, "I must. Please, sir, would you just leave us alone."

But this sport was too good to miss. He tethered his horse a few yards away and returned to the fray.

"If you are determined to help, please do so in the correct fashion," she said. "Do not lunge. We shall have to coax him. I should think that he is quite hungry now. I shall tempt him with this biscuit, and if you would take this sheet and toss it over him the moment he alights, we shall have him.''

The sun was warm, the air crisp, to the duke's delight chasing the bright red-and-green plumage through the park was most invigorating. Of course he fell twice, once landing in a thicket when he plunged a bit too late. And he got the feeling the bird enjoyed his plight, almost laughing at them as he led them through every thicket and bush in the damned park, and flapping his wings and cursing like a sailor in those blasted earsplitting squawks.

At last! A lucky toss of the sheet and the parrot was within his grasp. Winston sprawled on the ground and held on, wincing from the nasty scratch he had received from one vicious claw.

''Oh, thank you, sir,'' said the girl when she came to claim the devilish thing. At least, that was what he thought she said, for nothing could be heard but the damned screeching which was erupting through the sheet. ''Open hatches! Blast…blast…blast.'' He had no opportunity to introduce himself and ask her name.

She gave him no chance to speak, for she took the bird and hobbled off as fast as she could, considering that she wore but one shoe. He turned to search the ground. If he found the other one, he could follow to return it and discover her identity. ''A nobody,'' his mother had said. A damned intriguing nobody! He meant to better the acquaintance. He did not find the shoe, and, when he looked again, she had disappeared.

SHE WOULD HAVE LIKED to look for her shoe, but it was hard enough to keep the parrot secure. Besides, she was acutely embarrassed and anxious to make her escape. She had also recognized him as the man who had been carrying on with Jewel the night before, and at once. A duke—whatever was he doing in this part of Town? An idea pricked at her: had he come to meet Jewel?

But no. That thundering gallop had not been a prelude to a lovers' tryst, and she knew Jewel was still abed. She told herself to banish these unruly notions from her head. Flirtation was merely Jewel's way to make herself pleasing, no more than that.

"Oh, do be quiet, you wretch!" she said aloud, wishing she could stop the continuous barrage of squawks. "Just let me get you back to the house. You'll not escape again."

She should not have been rude to the man, for he had been a help, getting himself soiled and unkempt without a word of complaint. If she ever saw him again, which was an unlikely eventuality, she would apologise.

"Oh my Lord, miss!" wailed Mrs. Stokes when Amelia entered the house. "You ain't got on but one shoe! Oh, your poor papa."

"I lost it in the park, but it's quite an old one and—" She stopped, noticing the housekeeper's obvious distress. "But what on earth has my shoe to do with Papa?"

"'Walk with one shoe and you walk someone out of the family,'" Mrs. Stokes asserted solemnly. "And there's your poor papa, for all we know already on his deathbed. Laid out in a dead faint in his studio he was when Timothy found him, and—''

Amelia did not wait for more. She thrust the bird, surprisingly quiet now, at the woman and discarded her remaining shoe. Not that she credited such superstitions, but she did not want anything to impede her progress as she raced upstairs.

Her heart was beating wildly, but she entered the room quietly, not wishing to disturb her father. He was not asleep but lay on his bed, a damp cloth across his forehead. Jewel sat beside him, her face a mask of worry, one hand holding tightly to his.

''Oh, I'm glad you're back, Amelia,'' she said. ''Your papa fell in a faint in his studio and John brought him down and . . . Oh, I am so frightened.''

''Now do not get Amy all alarmed.'' Victor's voice sounded as jovial as usual, but a little weak. He tried to sit up, but Amelia pushed him gently back on the pillow.

''Lie still, Papa,'' she said, kneeling on the other side of the bed and stroking his arm. ''You must rest.''

''All of this fuss about nothing,'' he muttered.

''Nothing! And all of us scared out of our wits . . . swooning as you did.''

''Just a touch of the vapours, my dear.'' Victor actually smiled. ''Dashed womanish of me, I admit. But it was so hot and stuffy up there. I'm quite recovered now,'' he said, and insisted that he must get back to work.

"Indeed you will not," Amelia said, again restraining him as he started to rise. "Has the doctor been sent for?" she asked Jewel.

"John has gone to fetch him." Jewel took the cloth from Victor's head and dipped it into the bowl of vinegar water on the bedside table. "And you are not to move until Doctor Jones arrives," she told her husband, tenderly patting his face with the cloth before replacing it on his forehead. "It's just as I said, you have been working too hard."

The doctor confirmed her diagnosis. "Your father is suffering from a condition of languor," he told Amelia, "precipitated by neglect of the body and overwork of the mind. In his present state, I fear his work is too exacting and, compounded by the fumes from the paint pots and the Town air, may lead to a rupture of his entire system. I prescribe a long respite, in the country air, if possible."

For Victor, a long stay in the country was out of the question. He simply did not have the funds. However, all the household conspired to see that he was kept away from his studio and encouraged to rest at every opportunity. Even Jewel asserted herself to see to her husband's every comfort. Seeing this, Amelia began to develop a real appreciation of her stepmother.

"She really is caring for Papa," she said to Mrs. Stokes one day as they sorted out linens. "I'm so grateful she is able to keep him out of his studio."

"Suits that one just fine," Mrs. Stokes said with a sniff. "She always has been jealous of his paint pots and brushes taking up all his time. Now she has all his attention. All they do is ride or walk or play parlour games.''

"But that's just what Papa needs."

"Yes, missy, I know. And I grant you that right now that's all for the good." She sighed. "Never thought to be grateful for them teasing, pleasing ways of hers. Which is all she was raised for, come to think on it."

Amelia smiled as she inspected a worn napkin. "Surely no one is trained just to please."

"That one was. Her ma, you see, meant to make the most of them golden curls and great blue eyes. Though how she got the foolhardy notion that she could catch a member of the gentry for her daughter is more than I can see. She wasn't even likely to meet a gentleman. Her pa's inn was respectable enough, I suppose, but it never catered to the quality."

Amelia had heard the story before. She only half listened as Mrs. Stokes rattled on with the privilege of an old retainer and the vehemence of one who had adored her first mistress and resented the second.

"Well, the old lady died and I think her pa had quite given up. That one had plenty of admirers, you see, but weren't none of them offering marriage. Past six-and-twenty she was when Mr. Allen come along." Mrs. Stokes shook her head as she separated sheets. "As they say, there ain't no fool like an old one. Begging your pardon, Missy, but it seems your papa is more struck by beauty than most. And that one—well, she couldn't touch my Miss Venetia, but I must own she is quite lovely. And there's your papa, tall and handsome with those deep blue eyes, and not so old either. Five-and-forty, I think he was then. And lonely.

And never seeing harm in anyone. Well, he asked to paint her portrait. And I knew the first time I saw her tripping up those stairs how it was going to be. This house ain't been the same since—'' Mrs. Stokes broke off in a sudden surge of emotion.

"No, indeed. That one's nothing like your mama. Folks say Miss Venetia was silly, running off to marry an artist. But for all her charming and witty ways she had character and she was a real lady. Look at the way she took charge of this house. You know your papa ain't got no sense for all that he does no harm. But Miss Venetia right away weeded out the riffraff from the crowd that came traipsing in every night.''

Amelia was thoughtful as she gathered up the napkins which needed mending. She had been too young then to realize it, but when her mother was alive there had been gentility as well as conviviality in the groups that invaded the parlour each evening.

"And I'll tell you something else, miss,'' Mrs. Stokes said as Amelia made to depart. "Miss Venetia saw to the master's purse. We didn't have all those so-called guests hanging on his sleeve and she didn't spend every extra shilling on fripperies for herself.''

Amelia hurried away, feeling remorseful as she thought of how much had been spent on fripperies for herself.

"Good Lord, Amy, you look like a dowdy school ma'am,'' her father had declared the moment she returned home. And it was he, with his unerring good taste and unbounded generosity, who had insisted she be outfitted in the latest fashion by the best modiste. If she had only known . . .

But she had not, until her father became ill and she had to take over the accounts. She had suggested that Jewel do so, but that lady, who took no responsibility for anything, had demurred. "You best do it, my dear. I'm not at all good with figures."

It was not an easy task. Victor Allen was a respected and well-known artist and his portraits commanded a good sum. But, as he had no head for business, made no investments, and was careless about collections, his finances fluctuated precariously from one commission to the next. No finished portraits meant no commissions, and Amelia faced the burden of maintaining a very cumbersome household on an income rapidly diminishing to nothing.

How were they to manage? Her head was pounding with this thought as she went into the small drawing room and laid aside the napkins. She seated herself at her father's desk and took out pen and paper. In going over his papers she had found some accounts owing to him that were long overdue. She had begun writing small reminders requesting payment which she would have John deliver. However, she had small hope of recouping anything from this quarter, for his patrons usually paid immediately or not at all.

She paused, staring down at her pen, feeling suddenly weary. And frightened. Frightened for her father, so pale and thin and weak. He must have time to recover. Nothing must disturb him. She must keep things going!

But how? So many lives were dependent on him, not only herself and Jewel, but the servants: John, valet, butler, groom and general handyman; and Mrs.

Stokes, who really managed everything. Both she and John had been with the family since before Amelia was born. Even had she the heart to turn them out, where would they go? Her mind refused to focus on those others, whom Mrs. Stokes termed "spongers." Of course she had discontinued the evening gatherings, pleading that her father was ill and must have quiet. But what about the boarders, old Timothy and Rita, who had not secured a place with the touring company after all.

And the previous day, when Amelia returned from the market, she found a newcomer already installed in the small back bedroom: a sometime model for Victor, and sometime Shakespearean actress, who called herself Melody Harding. She seemed to regard the back bedroom as home, for she exclaimed, "So good to be home, my dear! 'Twas a most disappointing Season. Such a lack of culture these days—there's no appreciation for the Bard. So you are Victor's little daughter. How nice to have you with us, my dear. Poor Victor. Works too hard, you know. We must all rally round to care for him."

Amelia had been too disconcerted at the time to challenge her. Nor did she have that right. This was, after all, her father's house. But, she thought with some asperity, these three people were not his responsibility. If she were forced, as might be the case, to turn the house into a real boarding house, they would have to pay or make room for those who could.

John entered at that moment to announce that there was a gentleman wishing to see her.

"A gentleman? To see me?" She thought of the man who had helped her catch Sylvester and felt a flush burn her cheeks. Automatically she smoothed her hair as she took the card from John. "Henry Avery, Marquis of Chester." Not a duke. She ignored the prickle of disappointment. Still, the name meant nothing to her and she lifted a puzzled face to John.

"He has been here a few times in the evening, miss, and his man brought in a basket of fruit for Mr. Allen."

"Oh, that was kind."

"Yes, miss. Then his lordship asked to see you." John cleared his throat. "I said I would enquire if you were at home."

"Oh, John, how nonsensical! Of course I'm at home. Doubtless he wants to ask about Papa," she said as she went out.

He was standing before the fireplace and smiled as she came into the parlour. She recognized him at once. The man with the sandy hair and the roving eyes whose companion had addressed him as "Duckie."

"Lord Chester," she said, extending her hand. "How thoughtful of you to call."

"Miss Allen." He brushed her hand with his lips. "I have been concerned about your father. How is he?"

"Much improved, thank you. But he still requires rest and is unable to receive visitors just yet."

"I am glad he progresses. And of course I would not disturb him. It is you whom I wished to see."

"Oh?"

"I thought perhaps you might do me the honour of dining with me this evening." He seemed to sense her surprise and quickly added, "Or at another time, if tonight is inconvenient."

"Thank you, sir. But I must decline. With my father ill—" she spread her hands "—all my time is quite taken up."

"Surely not all your time!" he protested. His tone was persuasive and for a moment he seemed to hesitate. "I had thought... But no. I cannot wait." He drew a small velvet box from his pocket and opened it, displaying an emerald brooch so exquisite and so obviously valuable that she almost gasped. "The minute I saw this I was reminded of you. You must have it, for it reflects the colour of your beautiful eyes."

How dared he! "You are mistaken sir. My eyes are not that green," she replied, blushing with indignation.

"Ah, but they are, my dear," he said, oblivious of her seething displeasure. "As luminous and sparkling as—"

"In any case, I could not accept such a gift." She tried to keep her voice calm. "It is much too lavish."

He shrugged. "I am a very rich man, my dear. And," he added, giving her a meaningful look, "I am reputed to have a very generous nature."

"A well-deserved reputation, I am sure. My father will certainly enjoy your fruit."

"Ah, Miss Allen, you fail to understand."

"I understand you perfectly, sir. And, if I were a man, I'd call you out!"

"Ah, but if you were a man I'd not— Now, now, dear lady, no need to take offence." He stepped back, looking apprehensive. "I only wish to offer my help. I thought perhaps, under the circumstances—"

"My circumstances are not your concern. And, if we are to remain on good terms," she said sternly tugging at the bell pull, "pray say no more. I should like it very much if you would put that bauble back into your pocket and—" She turned to John who entered immediately. "The gentleman is leaving. Kindly throw...show him out." Turning on her heel, she swept from the room.

Lord Chester stared after her in stunned amazement. Then he looked down at the jewel in his hand. Never had he known a woman to refuse such a gift!

Amelia was furious but not surprised. This was not the first time she had been insulted in such a manner. There had been two other occasions when she had been subjected, though not as blatantly, to similar scenes. And what could she expect, living under Papa's roof? For a moment, her rage turned on her father and his utter disregard for propriety or appearances, his willingness to receive men and their mistresses as if they were respectable members of Society.

But only for a moment. She could not be angry at Papa, for a great part of his innate goodness was his unquestioning acceptance of everyone with no regard for, or judgement of, their conduct or consequence. She almost giggled as she returned to the desk to gather up her notes. If ever she did make a decision to become some gentleman's mistress, her father would probably only lift one eyebrow and enquire whether she would be happy doing so.

It simply would not occur to him that desperation alone might make a woman consider... She shook her head vehemently. Of course she would not consider such a thing! But she had been appalled to find that the first thought that had entered her head upon seeing the emerald was the price it would fetch. Such a sum would sustain their household for several months. For the first time she thought, if not with approval, at least with some understanding of the women who had chosen that path. If all one possessed was a bit of beauty and a way of pleasing...

"Oh, there you are, my dear." Jewel came in, looking very fetching in a Clarence blue walking dress. "I'm off to Hookham's to get some new reading material for Victor."

"Good," said Amelia. "He does like to hear you read."

"He's napping now, but... Well, I have a few other errands." Jewel concentrated on buttoning one smart leather glove. "I may be rather late. If you would look in on him..."

"Of course. I'll take my mending up and sit with him. But... An errand? Perhaps tomorrow when I go to market, I could—"

"Oh, no. I would not trouble you." Jewel hesitated, then said, "It's that new bonnet. I'm going to take it back to Madame Cecile. You did say we should make no purchases just now."

"Yes. So I did."

Her stepmother moved quickly towards the door, saying she would be back in time for supper.

"Jewel?"

"Yes?"

"The bonnet. Did you forget?"

"Oh, my!" Jewel looked down as if surprised that she held only her reticule. "How goosish of me! I vow I have just been at sixes and sevens since my poor Victor's upset. I'll fetch it right away." She hurried out and Amelia stared thoughtfully after her.

CHAPTER THREE

"It won't do, Miss Amelia." Old Timothy puffed hard on his pipe, an elegant object with a long curving stem and a magnificent seascape intricately scrimshawed on its large bowl, and squinted at the portrait of Lady Fitzgerald. "It won't do," he said again.

"Oh, I do wish you'd be done with saying that!" Still holding the brush in her hand, Amelia rubbed an arm across her damp brow and wrinkled her nose. "And must you smoke that pipe? Between those odious fumes and this heat—"

"Neither one got nothing to say to what you're doing to your pa's work." He leant forward and pointed his pipe stem at the canvas. "You've stirred up a storm in a calm, smooth sea!"

Shocked by his words, Amelia stepped back to survey her work. She couldn't have . . . Heavens, she had only added a few finishing touches, mostly to the face. And Papa himself had suggested it. Or had it been she?

She thought back to that afternoon when they had sat alone playing dominoes. She had been waiting for her father to take his turn, and when he didn't she looked up to see him frowning down at the pieces in his hand.

"Oh, you don't have a play!" she teased, laughing. "You'll have to pull from the pile, won't you?"

He looked so startled that she knew his mind was on something else.

"What is it, Papa?"

"I was thinking," he said, "that if I took the stairs slowly I might go up and finish that portrait of Lady Fitzgerald."

"Oh, no, Papa!" she cried in alarm. "It's not only the stairs. It's the work also. You know what the doctor said."

"I also know that the larder must be getting quite bare, child."

Amelia stirred uneasily. She had thought... But how could she think him unaware of their situation? No matter how carefree he appeared, it was he who had assumed all responsibility for this household for the many past years. It was not good for him to worry, and she tried to reassure him.

"We have enough to hold us for a while. And I discovered some accounts owing which you had overlooked. I sent round reminders."

His sceptical glance told her how much store he put in receiving money from those accounts. "Lady Fitzgerald's portrait is almost completed. All it needs is—"

"Papa, listen..." she had interrupted, and then put forth her plan. Yes, it had been she who suggested that she finish the portrait, but he had consented. And now Timothy was saying... Oh, what did he know! She picked up one of the sketches she had made earlier, studied it and looked again at the canvas.

"I think it will do very well," she said, almost to herself. "It's an exact likeness."

"And that's exactly why it *won't* do!" said Timothy. "Do you know why people want to sit for your pa, Miss Amelia?"

"Of course. Because he's an excellent artist."

Timothy shrugged. "That may be. But that ain't the reason. Thing is, he paints what he sees. And the blasted truth is, Victor's got a blind eye to whatever ain't right. He's so almighty good himself he can't see no flaws in anyone else."

"Timothy!" Amelia said in exasperation. "Will you stop all this roundaboutation and speak plain!"

Timothy hesitated, scratching his nose. Then he spoke out. "Well, missy, there's no denying that Lady Fitzgerald's a shrew. You can see it in them calculating eyes of hers. And there's no denying that you caught it—right there on that canvas!"

"Oh, you needn't go waving that pipe about as if I've committed some crime. I paint what I see!" she snapped. "Are you suggesting I should bow to your superior knowledge as a noted art critic and falsify—"

"I ain't no bloody expert and I ain't telling you how to paint. All I say is that what you see and what your pa sees are two different things. And that grand lady won't like what you see!"

"Well, you're no soothsayer, either, and you can't know what she'll like! Do stop hovering over me! Take that fancy, malodorous pipe and go back to your bones!'' She spoke crossly but, as old Timothy clomped back to his bench, she felt a deal more apprehension than anger. The horrible thought struck her that he might be right.

TWO DAYS LATER, Amelia anxiously watched Lady Fitzgerald, resplendent in a walking dress of purple broadcloth, ascend the stairs and move towards the canvas, her eyes alight with anticipation. She stopped before it and her eyes narrowed.

Amelia's heart beat a little faster.

Never taking her gaze from the portrait, Lady Fitzgerald stepped back and tilted her face from one side to the other. Then she moved forward again and, lifting her quizzing glass, bent to study the work more closely.

Amelia stood quietly, her lower lip held between her teeth. She almost bit it when Lady Fitzgerald suddenly wheeled about, her face contorted with rage.

''This is not me! Not in the least!'' she shrieked. ''Look at that mouth—and those eyes! Those are the eyes of a shrew.''

''I...I...that is—'' Amelia's stutter was cut short.

''Where is Mr. Allen? Summon him immediately! I was led to expect better from him and I shall not hesitate to tell him so!''

''I . . . I'm sorry. My father is ill and cannot—''

''Ill? Then possibly that explains this shoddy work!'' Lady Fitzgerald bristled with indignation, as if Victor's illness had been timed to spoil her portrait. She voiced her displeasure in infinite detail before she flounced out, announcing that she was not about to pay out good money for a picture that was not a proper likeness.

"Never mind, child. It's not your fault," Victor told his dismayed daughter. "No need to get into a pucker. Lady Fitzgerald is a mite hard to please. And all is not lost. I'll put it to rights as soon as I am well."

He had appeared so calm as he tried to soothe her. Only later did she learn how truly anxious he was. For the next morning, when both she and Jewel were out, he had John assist him to the attic. There, attempting to put Lady Fitzgerald to rights, he suffered a relapse. The doctor was summoned again and Victor was returned to bed.

Now Amelia was more worried than ever. She knew that he would not be able to rest and recover until convinced that his household was secure. Amelia was desperate. Not only had she counted on the commission from Lady Fitzgerald's portrait, but had contemplated finishing two others from her father's sketches. Now she dared not attempt it.

However, some temporary relief did come, for two of Amelia's reminders bore fruit. Sir Aubrey Canfield sent his apologies for the delay and a draft for one hundred pounds in payment of his granddaughter's portrait, completed six months before. Another partial payment of twenty-five pounds arrived from a Mrs. Sinclair, and one morning Timothy slipped ten pounds into her hand, saying he had sold some of his scrimshaws and wanted to share the profits with Victor.

Amelia, considerably relieved, was pondering ways to stretch this unexpected bounty when the letter came.

It was from a solicitor at Covington Corners, Sussex, and it was addressed to her. Amelia stared in some perplexity before she broke the seal and unfolded the pages.

> My dear Miss Allen:
>
> It is with extreme regret that I must inform you of the death of your uncle, Sir Cyrus Fielding, on the 15th inst. as a result of a hunting accident.
>
> Reading of His Last Will and Testament will occur at Farsdale promptly at two of the clock, the afternoon of May thirtieth of this year. Should it prove impossible for you to be present, please inform this office immediately as it is imperative that all beneficiaries attend.
>
> The favour of an early reply is humbly requested. I remain,
>
> > Your Obedient Servant
> > J. R. Brown, Esq.

"FARSDALE? But, Guy, my dear boy, you have just returned to London," said the duchess. "Must you be off to this . . . what is it? Fernhall?"

"Farsdale. And, yes, I must." The Duke of Winston smiled at his mother and tried not to look at the clock. He had been on the verge of departing for his club when his mother, accompanied by the paunchy Lord Linton, had unexpectedly arrived at the small quarters he still maintained at Ramsay Place.

"Then you must delay your departure," she said decisively. She tapped Linton's arm lightly with her fan. "Did I not tell you how it would be? Now you understand why I had to see Guy myself rather than sending a messenger.''

"Yes, my dear," Linton agreed, his eyes fastening appreciatively on the duchess.

And it was no wonder, Guy thought. His mother was still a handsome woman, tall and regal with a smooth complexion and only a hint of grey in her auburn hair.

Now she turned from Linton and waved the fan at her son. "It is absolutely imperative that you be here tomorrow night, for I have arranged a small dinner party before we set off for the theatre. An intimate gathering, just Linton and the Courtlands.''

"Quite a cosy group, and surely to be spoiled by my presence.''

"Don't be nonsensical! The Courtlands will be accompanied by their daughter, Deborah, Lord Granville's widow, you know. You two ought to become better acquainted.''

"Good Lord!'' he croaked. "I've known Deborah since I was in knee britches and I've no wish to better the acquaintance.''

"Now, Guy, you must listen to me. It is well past time for you to be considering—'' She broke off as Driscol, his manservant, appeared, bearing a tray. She sat on a sofa and occupied herself with arranging her silk shawl while Driscol poured ratafia for herself and port for the gentlemen. Linton, who was also in evening attire, for they were on their way to a ball, seated himself beside her.

"Thank you,'' she said as she took her glass from Driscol. She observed the manservant carefully and, after he left the room, spoke with asperity. "That man is positively untidy. I am persuaded he just scrambled into his coat when he heard us at the door. He certainly has not the proper appearance for a . . . a footman," she concluded, evidently in doubt as to Driscol's position.

"He serves me well," said the Duke amicably, as he leaned against the mantel and sipped his port. He had no intention of replacing Driscol, who had been his ever-alert batman during those dangerous months on the Peninsula.

"And these quarters cannot be adequate." The duchess glanced about the room. "Really, Guy, I can't imagine why you remain here when—"

"Now, Mama, my love, we've been through all that before. I'm quite comfortable." He prided himself that since his father's death the year before, he had admirably conducted all the business of the estate he had inherited. But he refused to be saddled with all its trappings. He was more than glad to have his mother preside over Winston Hall and all the social pomp and ceremony connected with it.

"Well, be that as it may," said his mother, "about tomorrow night—you must be there."

"Impossible. I leave for Farsdale early on the morrow."

"But why must you go? And at this particular time?"

"A debt of honour, ma'am."

"Oh, you men and your debts of honour," she flared. "I daresay it's some nonsensical wager, endangering your fortune or your life."

"It's not that sort of debt, Mama, though it does rather involve my life. At least it did. This chap took a bullet meant for me—at some cost to himself."

"Oh? On the field of battle?" Linton looked up with interest. "A fellow officer?"

"Yes." The duke set his glass on the mantel and told them. For a long moment he was back on the battlefield, his lungs thick with the smell of blood and gunpowder, hearing the whiz of bullets, the cries of wounded men and the frenzied neighing of frightened horses. He hadn't realized he was in the line of fire until Fielding had slammed against him, pulling them both to the ground—a split second too late, for Fielding had taken the bullet himself.

"Was it fatal?" asked Lord Linton.

"No, thank goodness. But he was severely wounded. We managed to get him to the field surgeon and it was touch and go for a time. Feverish, and fearing he was on his deathbed, he rambled on incessantly about who would inherit his property. He seemed anxious that it remain in the family. Finally he rallied enough to dictate a will, requesting, and I of course agreed, that I become trustee and take on some charges pertaining to the inheritance."

Lord Linton nodded approvingly. "He had saved your life. You owed whatever he asked."

The duchess only seemed annoyed. "You say his wound was not fatal. Why are you concerned now?"

"No, not fatal," the duke answered. "And I thought that would be the end of it. He said he intended to make out a new will when and if he married, and I would be relieved of the charge. That was more than two years ago, and I was sure the happy event had occurred. But when I returned yesterday, I found a letter from some solicitor informing me that Fielding had expired from injuries received in a hunting accident and requesting that I be present for the reading of the will, which I gather has not been changed. To be there in time I must leave early tomorrow.''

''Oh, dear! How provoking!'' the duchess exclaimed. ''There surely has been time in two years for him to marry and change his will. Oh, now, do not frown so. Of course I am indeed sorry for the poor man. But it is so inconvenient that he should die now and take you from London in the middle of the Season!''

The duke's mouth twisted wryly, and Lord Linton observed that the ''poor man'' must also have considered the event untimely. ''Not in his dotage, was he?''

''Oh, no,'' said the duke. ''Two-and-thirty I think, only four years older than myself. I was sorry to hear of his accident.''

''Young people do take such ridiculous chances,'' his mother said as she stood. ''Come along, Linton. We must be on our way. And, Guy, promise me you'll not take a fancy to join some dangerous hunting expedition but will return to London straightaway. And take your travelling coach. Don't go racing off recklessly in your curricle. And remember to take your riding cloak. I shouldn't like you to take a chill.''

Later that evening as he joined his cousin, Baron Humphrey, at his club, the duke remarked that he didn't know which worried his mother most, the possibility of his early demise or the improbability of his impending marriage.

"Both," said Lord Humphrey. "You know Aunt Phoebe dotes on you, and she'd be sorely stricken by your sudden death. In the meantime, she'd surely be happy to see you suitably leg shackled to a lady of her choice. Time you produced an heir, old fellow," he said, as he picked up his cards.

"Ah, but I have an heir—you."

"Well, I hope you don't think I'm so bacon-brained as to want the job."

"Job? Station, my boy, station! Must give the title proper respect." The duke looked at his cards, discarded three and drew three from the deck. "I hope you realize, Lewis, that, as the tenth Duke of Winston, you'd be—"

"Spending half my time in Parliament, and saddled with all those cursed estates and the whole blasted family forever pulling on me! No, thank you. Come to think of it, Guy, didn't I see cousin Harry driving your curricle the other day?"

"You might have."

"Damned if I'd let him have mine."

"Just let him have the curricle, not my bays." The duke grinned as he pinched his nose. "Thought I'd got off lightly with the loan of the curricle and a monkey. Are you ever going to play, Lewis?"

"Patience, my boy, patience!" Lord Humphrey carefully studied his hand, then leisurely discarded one card and drew one from the deck, saying as he did so, "Cousin Harry. Now there's one who would not hesitate to accede to the title. Which I grant would be a pity, for he'd soon have the whole lot in the sponging house."

"True. So it is a fortunate circumstance that he's so far distant on the family tree that succession is quite out of his reach."

"I must say even though I'm next in line, your mama don't think much of the idea. She ain't got too much against me, to be sure. I wager it's my Hilda."

"Hilda?"

"Lord, yes. Can't you see my Hilda as the Duchess of Winston? She'd be lording it over everyone and properly putting Aunt Phoebe sadly out of curl."

"Stuff and nonsense, Lewis. Mama's always urging me to marry and she'd be in the same position if my wife—"

"Not if you married a biddable girl like Elise Worthington or Courtland's milksop daughter. She's a widow now, you know. In either case, your mama would still rule the roost. Now with my Hilda... there'd be quite a dust-up. There," he said, spreading his hand to rake in the duke's guineas, "at this rate I might *win* your fortune. Your deal."

The duke smiled as he shuffled the cards. "You just might have a point, old chap. Mama's been pushing Elise Worthington at me for days. And she's got a plan to throw me in the way of Courtland's daughter tomorrow night."

"Ah!"

"Well, I'm escaping that noose. I'm off for Farsdale tomorrow morning. Saddled with a charge I'd like to avoid."

"Oh?"

"No matter. I'll just turn the whole business over to Casper. A word to you, cousin. Should you be unfortunate enough to step into my shoes, leave everything to Casper. You couldn't wish for a better man of business."

"Back to that," said Humphrey as he picked up his cards. "Maybe you should consider Elise Worthington. Pretty little thing even if she is a milk and water miss. You surely don't want to choose a woman like Hilda."

"Thank you. But I'm not choosing at the moment. I'll just let you and Mama stew over my possible early demise. Of course I'm not contemplating that, either, at the moment." He stared at the cards in his hand. "Incidentally, Lewis, at the Stewart ball the other night there was a rather striking redhead. Would you know—"

"Sorry, Guy, but Hilda prevents my observing any striking women. And among the ton I haven't noticed any striking redheads lately." He gave his cousin a sharp glance. "Do I detect a spark of interest in that quarter? Are we in for a duchess with red hair?"

"Good Lord! I simply made an enquiry and I'm hauled off to the altar! And by you, cousin!" He pointed a finger at Lord Humphrey. "Just how many beauties have paraded through that love nest of yours?"

"Touché!" Humphrey laughed. "But there was a look in your eyes that… All right. All right. I was only thinking."

"Well, stop thinking." The duke put down his cards and stood up. "I concede. I must be off, as I plan to get away early tomorrow."

As he drove home, he found he could not stop thinking of the redhead with the flashing green eyes. Not as a duchess, however. Oh, she had the look of one but certainly not the temperament. A beauty most certainly, but a spitfire.

Gad! She put him in mind of one of his mistresses. What was her name? Ah...Lucinda. She had been prone to pelt him with whatever cutlery was at hand whenever he roused her displeasure. But damned if she hadn't been the best bed partner he'd ever had. He had almost regretted it when she passed from his arms to those of Lord Prentice.

Ah, yes. When he returned to London he planned to seek out that redhead. She had the beauty and fire to warm a man's blood.

FARSDALE. Amelia again perused the letter. She knew, of course, that her mother's home had been called Farsdale. Also that there had been a much younger brother.

Her mother had been disowned, cast off. Bitterness swelled within her as she thought how her mother had been ignored all these years. Beautiful, vivacious Venetia, so loving and kind, abandoned by her family. What kind of people were they?

Still the bitterness could not quell a kindling anticipation. The family, as she understood it, had been moderately wealthy. Could they have left her...as much as . . . goodness, even as much as a thousand pounds?

Oh, she must not arouse false hopes.

But it was possible.

She must go. She would have to use some of the precious money she had just received to travel. How far and how much? Mail was probably cheaper than stage. And did she dare go alone?

CHAPTER FOUR

"GOOD NEWS, PAPA!" Amelia cried as she ran into Victor's room and handed him the letter. "At least I think it is good." Surely the mysterious J. R. Brown, esquire would not require her to travel all the way to Farsdale for a few shillings.

Jewel put down her book and stood behind her husband's chair to peer over his shoulder. Her lips moved silently as she read. Then her blue eyes widened and her face took on an expression of surprise, expectation and greed as she read aloud the last few lines. Mrs. Stokes, who was placing the tea tray on the low table, lingered to listen.

"What do you think, Papa?" Amelia asked. "Shall I go?"

"Of course you must go, you silly goose!" Jewel cried. "And in haste! Dear me ... what day are we today? The tenth. And you must be there by ... Heavens, you have only five days! You must pack immediately. I'll help you." She put her hands to her face, then waved them excitedly. "This is providential! Beyond anything. Such good fortune. Providence, Victor. Now, I suppose you must go by stage. Such a pity we have no travelling coach. Mrs. Stokes, fetch John and tell him to enquire about the stage."

But the housekeeper remained bent over the table, her hands busy arranging scones, milk and sugar while she watched Victor out of the corner of her eye. Amelia's eyes also remained fixed on her father, as she puzzled at the faraway look, the pain reflected in his face.

"What is wrong, Papa? Do you not wish me to go?"

"Don't be nonsensical! Of course he wants you to go." Jewel bristled with impatience. "Mrs. Stokes, do stop fiddling with that tea and fetch John!" One hand flew up in agitation. "Oh, I do recall he's gone to the smith about that axle! Do send him to me the minute he returns. Now, Victor, you are not to worry. I'll arrange everything. Come, Amelia, we must see to your wardrobe. I think you should travel in that black brocade. Yes, black…appropriate in your time of grief."

Amelia was still watching her father, who had not spoken. It was as if he had forgotten their presence.

"Amelia!" Jewel turned, her hand on the doorknob, her voice urgent. "Do come now! We have no time to dally."

It was a significant nod from Mrs. Stokes that made Amelia reluctantly follow her stepmother. As the door shut behind them, Amelia could hear the housekeeper's gentle voice.

"Here, take your tea, sir. Best you drink it while it's hot."

Obediently he drank the hot, strong brew, swallowing it in great gulps, as if it might ward off the chill of past memories.

"She must go, sir." Mrs. Stokes said.

"I don't want her to be hurt."

"There's no one to hurt her now. Cyrus...he was the last." A sob caught in her throat and a tear rolled down her weatherbeaten cheek.

Victor reached up to take her hand. "Sit down, Mrs. Stokes. And pour yourself a cup of tea."

Gratefully she sank into a chair as if to relieve the weight of her sorrow. His heart welled with pity for this warmhearted woman who had known his Venetia all her life, who had grieved with him for her, as she was grieving now for Venetia's brother. Her tea grew cold as she began to talk.

"Imagine. He come safe through that dreadful war. And now...to succumb to a hunting accident. Always was reckless, you know, even as a lad. Lord, he'd jump them hedges easy as you please. Headstrong and happy." She paused. "Farsdale was a happy place."

Victor glanced at her and put down his cup. "They made my poor Venetia unhappy. Casting her off as they did."

"Poor Venetia, indeed! She did not spend an unhappy minute in her life...putting aside that time she fancied herself crossed in love by that perfidious duke." Mrs. Stokes lifted her head defiantly. "And there was no casting off. She simply left. You know how strong-willed she was. And it was right and good that she did, for she fell straight into your arms to spend the happiest twenty years a body could hope for."

The happiest years. Victor shut his eyes. He saw her as clearly as if she were standing there before him: that cloud of red hair, those green eyes twinkling one moment with merriment, in another, flashing with rage or determination, or brimming with tears. "Hearts do not break," he had told her, "they sting and ache." As his did . . . even yet. He could not stop the longing for her. He stirred uneasily in his chair. It was so unfair to Jewel. But he couldn't seem to help it.

"Cyrus was just a boy then. He hardly knew his sister." Mrs. Stokes sighed. "But he must have thought of her and remembered her child in his will."

"Can't be much," Victor said, and hated himself for resenting whatever had been left her, hated himself that he couldn't provide as he always had for his own, that she needed whatever she would be given by an uncle she didn't even know. "He probably left a wife and children . . . heirs."

"More'n likely." The housekeeper nodded. "But missy has a right to see the place where her mother grew up. And a right to know her cousins and her heritage."

Her only heritage. He had never really minded that his own had been snatched from him . . . his title, his lands. When he was eleven years old, it had all been an adventure. The narrow escape from the guillotine. The perilous journey through back roads and forests as, disguised as peasants, he, his mother and Jean, his faithful valet, made their way through the French countryside and across the Channel. A different country, a new life, another adventure. Victor Auguste Alain, Marquis de Beauchante of France became plain Victor Allen of England, without regrets.

But his child?

"Missy has a right," Mrs. Stokes said again. And so he agreed to let her go.

AMELIA HAD NOT EXPECTED the preparations for her journey to be so complicated. First and foremost, Papa stipulated that she was not to travel alone. So someone had to accompany her. But who?

Not Jewel, or John, who were both indispensable to Papa. Not Mrs. Stokes, without whom the household would fall apart.

It was Melody Harding who came to the rescue. "Put yourself at ease, Victor dear," she said, assuming an air of regal command and speaking with ringing authority. "Fortunately, I am between engagements and can come to your aid in this hour of need. How providential that I am at leisure and can accompany your daughter."

Victor opened his mouth, then closed it, as if unable or unwilling to express his opinion.

"Ah, now, my friend, do not let my youthfulness distress you." The reluctantly aging actress tilted her head coquettishly. "I am well versed in the thespian art and can easily contrive the manner of a proper companion despite my youthful appearance."

"Which ain't all that youthful, despite all her art with them ointments and powders." Mrs. Stokes declared privately to Amelia as they filled her portmanteau. "And she ain't all that proper neither. But she is a great one for aping the Quality so she may pull it off. Now, missy, hadn't we better pack this green dinner gown?"

"Indeed you must not!" said Jewel who bustled in at that moment. "Nor that light blue walking dress. Here's a black one of mine which you may have to tuck in a bit, Mrs. Stokes."

"Please don't bother," said Amelia. "I vow I'll not wear crape for an uncle I never knew in life." But, try as she would, she could not convince Jewel that her legacy, which had already been decreed by the deceased, would not be altered one whit by the wearing of mourning dress. Indeed, Jewel seemed to be mortally afraid that the legacy might be snatched from her, should Amelia not appear in attire denoting grief for the dear departed, or indeed if she did not arrive in a conveyance suitable to receive the large inheritance which increased with each of Jewel's imaginings. Jewel had decided that to go by stage would never do.

"You'll be set down at some common inn and you will have to hire some hackney to convey you to Farsdale. And what kind of conveyance would you find in such an out-of-the-way place? More than likely a common gig driven by some farmer and drawn by his workhorse! And how would that look?"

"It would look like something we could pay for," answered Amelia, who had been trying in vain to convince Jewel of the necessity for frugality, while at the same time shielding Victor from such disquieting discussions. She was in the drawing room, arguing this point with her stepmother and Melody, who tended to side with Jewel, when a visitor was announced.

"Lord Chester," said John. "He's had a bit of luck with the hunting and says he has brought over the plumpest of the covey in hopes of tempting Mr. Allen's delicate palate." John coughed. "He enquired after the ladies of the house."

"Oh, do show him in," cried Jewel before Amelia could speak. When he appeared, she rushed forward to greet him. "Lord Chester, how nice of you to call. And thank you. You are always so kind to Victor."

"I am very fond of Victor," the Marquis said as he bent over her hand. "And you, Miss Allen, I hope you are well," he said, turning to Amelia.

"Very well, thank you." Amelia spoke with cool civility and moved a little away.

He appeared not to notice and made his courtesies to Melody, who smiled and blinked and held out her hand with exaggerated dignity.

"How providential that you are here," said Jewel. "Would you advise us?"

"If it should be in my power to do so, ma'am."

"We are in such a quandary! Here is the difficulty, your lordship. My stepdaughter has just inherited a large fortune." Jewel spread her hands to indicate the enormity of it. "But she must travel to Farsdale to collect it. That is located somewhere in the vicinity of Covington Corners, a journey of two, perhaps three, days, which the shatter-brained child proposes to make by stage. I tell her this is no time to be so clutch-fisted."

"Pray desist, ma'am," Amelia, acutely embarrassed, begged. "Our problems are of no concern to Lord Chester."

"On the contrary, dear lady. Any problem of yours is of the greatest concern to me." He looked directly at Amelia, who averted her eyes.

"Of course," said Jewel. "Don't be so missish, Amelia. Lord Chester is a dear friend and will be glad to advise us. Pray be seated, sir. I'll have John bring in some refreshment." This duly attended to, she seated herself on the sofa beside Lord Chester. Melody sat across from them.

Amelia stood by the window, deploring Jewel's compulsion to indulge in frenzied flirtation each time she was in the presence of a handsome man. Lord Chester was handsome enough, despite the signs of dissipation that clouded his grey eyes. And of course he was titled! Amelia gave the drapery cord a vicious twist and winced as she listened to Jewel's obsequious drivel.

"You are a man of the world, your lordship, and you must have had wide experience, travelling about to all sorts of places. I'm sure you know what is best. Do give us your opinion." She leaned forward confidingly. "You see, it is quite impossible for me to abandon my poor Victor. Dear Miss Harding has kindly consented to go in my place." She gestured towards Melody, who blinked and nodded. "But I must be assured that they travel in safety. Don't you agree, sir, that it would be best to hire a chaise here in London, with a well-recommended coachman, to convey them to Farsdale and back?"

"No, madam, I do not," he said. Amelia, somewhat relieved at this statement, turned to look at him. He smiled at Jewel and held up a hand to halt her protestations of alarm. "Hear me out, madam. There is no need to hire a vehicle. Not when my travelling coach, with coachmen and groom, stands ready to serve you for as long as you may require."

"Oh, Lord Chester! How kind!" Jewel clasped her hands in rapture. "And how generous. Victor will be so pleased. And indeed I am grateful. Such a relief! We can never thank you enough. You cannot know how—"

"Jewel, please!" Amelia cut short the fawning. "It is kind of you, Lord Chester. But I thank you, no. I would not wish to inconvenience you."

"Nonsense. I have no plans to travel. My coach is standing idle."

"And I am sure we can manage very well without it." She moved from the window to face them. "Really, sir, I do not wish to be under any obliga—" She caught herself, and coughed. "That is, we prefer not to borrow."

"Oh, my dear, do consider!" Melody, who for a moment had been struck dumb by Amelia's refusal, now felt compelled to intervene. "An excellent philosophy. As the Bard says, 'Neither a borrower, nor a lender be.'" She smiled coyly at Lord Chester, then rose to clutch at Amelia's sleeve. "Unless we are in desperate need, which indeed we are. And you understand that, don't you, sir?" she asked, turning back to Lord Chester, who put down his wineglass and stood to face Amelia.

"I do understand. And I will not have you subjected to the inconveniences of stage travel."

"And subjected to...to...all kinds of things." Jewel was now also on her feet and said entreatingly, "Amelia, you don't understand how it will be. Two defenceless women travelling alone in the company of, and subject to, the advances of common tradesmen and the other riffraff upon whose patronage these commercial carriers depend!''

''Piffle!'' said Amelia. ''I assure you we will be in no danger, ma'am.''

''Ah...such innocence! We must ever be on guard, my dear.'' Melody placed a hand dramatically upon her bosom and sighed. ''Beauty, seen as a blessing, can often be a curse!''

''Piffle!'' Amelia repeated, then turned to Lord Chester. ''Thank you again, sir, but we must decline. It is best that we go by stage. Good day, your lordship.'' She left the room, putting an end to the discussion.

However, that did not end the matter. Lord Chester made his offer to Victor who, concerned for Amelia's safety, and convinced that the offer arose out of friendship, accepted. And Amelia, who did not like to disabuse him of his notion, acquiesced.

When Lord Chester came to see them off, Amelia, determined that he should be under no false illusions, said quite pointedly, ''My father thanks you for this favour extended to him and hopes to repay you as soon as he is well. Possibly with a portrait of one of your...that is, any lovely lady of your choice.''

He seemed to ignore the implication, for there was a significant look in his sleepy grey eyes as he replied, ''No need for that, my dear. One warm smile from you is repayment enough.''

''Good day, sir,'' she said, her face set and severe.

She should have smiled, she thought a trifle remorsefully, as the travelling coach pulled off and she sank back against the squabs. This was infinitely more comfortable than being in a close stage, squeezed among perfect strangers. How convenient to travel in a private chaise with a coachman and groom who would bespeak accommodations at inns. She felt happy. Papa was improving, and it was quite possible that this legacy might sustain them until he had completely recovered. Melody, though admittedly a bit rough around the edges, had an engaging wit and lively humour which made her an excellent travelling companion. Amelia settled back to enjoy the trip.

THE DUKE OF WINSTON arrived at Covington Corners and put up at the White Hart, the only inn in the town, and not up to his usual standards. But what could be expected in this out-of-the-way place? They had travelled at a rapid pace, as was his custom, stopping only to change horses, and it had been a rather tiresome trip. Leaving his man to make his arrangements, the duke decided to stretch his limbs by walking through the village and along the country lanes.

As he again neared the inn shortly before the dinner hour, he moved aside to allow a smart travelling coach to pass. Very smart indeed, he thought, glancing at the crest on the door.

Chester! By gad! What the devil was *he* doing so far off the main road? No matter. Chester was a jolly fellow, always good for dicing or cards. Good. He might not spend such a dull evening after all.

The carriage stopped at the inn, and when the groom opened the door two fashionably dressed ladies emerged. Winston was able only to catch a quick glimpse before they disappeared into the inn. But he knew Chester's taste in travelling companions. He chuckled to himself. If these two ran true to form he could expect a lively evening indeed.

He looked about for Chester but saw no sign of him. Perhaps he followed on horseback. The duke shrugged, took the steps and entered the inn. The women stood with their backs to him while their groom conversed with the innkeeper. As the door shut behind him, the one nearest turned round.

He stopped short, drawing a quick breath as his eyes took in the trim figure in the black travelling outfit.

By gad! Fate was lavishing her good will upon him! For the third time this month he was facing the comely redhead with the bewitching green eyes. And the eyes were not flashing. They held only smiling surprise!

Thinking himself the luckiest of fools, he moved quickly forward and bent over her extended hand, enjoying its softness and the fresh scent of lavender. "Dear lady, we meet again. Such a surprise!"

"Yes, isn't it?" she said. "So unexpected. And our last meeting was such a...well, I fear I was rude. You were so helpful and I promised myself I'd thank you if ever we met again, which then seemed most unlikely. And...oh, dear. We haven't been introduced."

"Ah, but we were. Don't you remember? By a friend—Sylvester, wasn't it? A most loquacious friend, arrayed in extremely fine feathers."

"Oh, yes. So he was. Very colourful feathers." Her gurgle of laughter was low and he found himself enchanted. "And you are right. Sylvester tends to be rather...talkative. And loud. Oh, excuse me," she said as the other woman, voluptuous in close fitting pelisse, touched her arm.

"I'm sorry my dear, but we shall have to share a bedchamber," she said.

"That's quite all right," answered the intriguing redhead.

"But it seems there is only one private parlour which has been spoken for," said the woman in the pelisse. "And I daresay it was spoken for by you," she added, turning to the duke and coyly wagging her finger at him. "Naughty man! I am persuaded you did so on purpose."

"I...that is..." He hesitated, staring at the woman and wondering why she looked so familiar. Those slanting dark eyes, the high cheekbones—he had seen them somewhere. He tried to remember where as he stuttered, "I had no idea you would have need of it. I—"

"Of course you didn't. And it's quite all right. Good day, sir. Come, Melody, we shall have dinner in our chamber." She took a firm hold on her friend's elbow and tried to pull her away. But Melody had no intention of leaving. Amelia was forced to apply more pressure than she would have liked.

Melody. Melody. He had heard the name before. Where? Oh, what the deuce! It was the other who mattered.

"One moment, please," he begged. "I would not deprive you of the parlour. In fact, I should be delighted to have you dine with me."

"Oh, now, isn't that kind, Amelia? Sir, you are a gentleman and we should be delighted—"

But the duke was still in a muse. *Amelia.* So that was her name.

"No!" said Amelia sharply. "I thank you, sir. But we will do very well in our chamber."

"And deny me the pleasure of your company? For shame! I was so looking forward to an enjoyable evening with you."

"Thank you. But we have not really been introduced, you know."

"Sylvester—"

"Sylvester doesn't count, I'm afraid."

Why was the devilish woman being so contrary!

Chester, thought Winston, rather belatedly. "You are travelling with Lord Chester, are you not?"

"No. We are quite on our own," said Amelia.

"But we know him," put in Melody, and prattled on despite all Amelia's frantic efforts to discourage her. "Lord Chester is a friend...a very dear friend. And besides, I know you, your grace. And don't pretend you don't remember me, even if it was two years ago. We had such fun," she said, rolling her eyes provocatively.

Good God! Where?

"Ah...yes...it was at..." He floundered, trying desperately to remember.

"It was at Lord Finmore's country house," she supplied. "I was in the company of Lord Eaton."

"Er, yes." He nodded slowly, remembering. One of those house parties he had quite tired of: lots of wine and games and blind man's buff with a horde of indecently clad lightskirts. And yes, this was the one that had hung on Eaton's arm. "Of course. How good to see you again," he said quickly. "Would you do me the honour of presenting me to your friend?"

Melody graciously performed the introduction. Even so, they had difficulty persuading Amelia, and it was some time before she reluctantly agreed that they should dine with him.

Upstairs in his room he reflected upon the strange meeting as he changed for dinner. Where were they going? And why in Lord Chester's coach?

The one who had most recently been seen on Eaton's arm had called him "a dear friend." And Eaton: now, what had he heard about him? Debts? A duel? Something that had made him flee the country. And had this Melody been passed on to Lord Chester?

No, by gad! If he knew Chester, it was the redhead who was the dear, dear friend! He threw down his towel with an oath, utterly surprised by the hot wave of anger racing through him.

Good Lord, what was the matter with him? Not the thing for him to care a jot for mistresses who passed from one protector to another. And what if she were under Chester's protection? It wouldn't be the first time he had snatched a mistress from another gentleman. Chester didn't deserve her, by gad!

CHAPTER FIVE

"MELODY, DEAR, I do wish you had not been so forward," Amelia said as soon as they were alone in their bedchamber. "It appeared ... Well, that is, we appeared not quite the thing." She hesitated, conscious that she might have been a bit forward herself. She had been so surprised to see him and yet grateful for the opportunity to apologise and thank him properly.

"Not quite the thing?" Melody glanced at her in alarm. "Was my wig slipping?"

"No, no. Truly. You looked fine."

"Well, thank goodness for that." Melody took off her hat and laid it on the bureau. "But what has you in such a taking?"

"I am just tired from the travel." Amelia faltered. "Nothing to signify."

"Best to keep smart, dearie. Imagine meeting a duke—here, of all places! This ain't exactly a quality inn."

"True," Amelia agreed. It was strange, encountering him in such a remote area. "I daresay he's off to some hunting lodge or some such. One can't always choose a proper stopping place."

"Well, ain't it lucky he stopped here tonight. And we, as smart as you please—bang up to the mark!"

Melody peered into the small mirror and fondly touched her burnished array of false curls. "Woman's crowning glory. Worth every guinea. How one looks is everything, my dear. Everything!"

"Not quite. One's behaviour counts for something." Amelia hung up her pelisse and slipped off her black skirt. "Melody, I am persuaded you inveigled that man into asking us to dine with him."

"Of course I did. You didn't really wish to eat here, did you?" She gestured at the tiny chamber, now cluttered with their belongings. "But it didn't take much inveigling. Didn't you see how he gaped at you?"

"Oh, Melody!" Amelia bent over the wash-basin to hide her heightened colour. *Had* he looked at her in a certain way?

"I ain't imagining it, dearie. Eaton looked at me like that the first time I clapped eyes on him. He was standing at the stage entrance of the Orpheum when I come out. 'Miss Harding,' he says. 'Will you do me the honour of dining with me?' 'Sir,' I says, 'I don't believe I've made your acquaintance.' Don't do to appear too easy, you know. But I'd seen that diamond pin in his cravat and I wasn't about to let that fish get away. So I let him persuade me. Best step I ever took was into his carriage."

"Well...yes, perhaps," Amelia said rather dubiously. "But, Melody, you do see that this situation is quite different."

"Nothing different about it. As old as Adam and Eve. Let me give you a bit of advice, dearie. Follow the gleam."

"The gleam?"

"In that man's eyes. Because it reflects gold. Eaton said Winston was one of the warmest men in England. Much richer than Chester, m'dear."

"All of which means nothing to me," Amelia replied, quite exasperated. "I'd not like you to be under any misapprehension. Lord Chester is . . . is only a friend. Please understand that."

"Oh, I do, dearie. And they do say a bird in the hand is worth two in the bush. But think on it." Melody's brow furrowed as if she were considering the odds. "If the bird in the bush is prodigiously plump and begging to be plucked . . . Now, don't look at me like that, dearie. The duke could be in your pocket in a trice. I'll tell you how to go on."

"But I don't want to go on! That is, I know how."

"Of course you do, dearie. And I'll help you. I know all about it. Eaton was that heel over ears before he knew what he was about!" Melody shrugged her arms into the sleeves of a red satin dinner dress. "Give me a hand with these buttons, will you, dear?"

"Oh, will you stop prattling on about this duke!" Amelia was so exasperated that she fumbled with the buttons. "I shall be perfectly clear about this. I have no desire to attach him and I certainly should not like to give him that impression!"

"Precisely! It wouldn't do to let him know you're that eager. Now, if you—"

"Stop! I'll not listen to another word of this." It was useless, Amelia thought, to try to make her understand. She only hoped that the silly woman would behave with some decorum at dinner. "And Melody," she added rather hesitantly. "Please, dear, at dinner... well, do be mindful of your manners."

"Oh, never fear about my manners. I know how to get on with the nobility, being often among them, you see, when I was with Eaton." She gave the skirt of her dress a shake. "And don't get into a pucker. I've had vast experience with men, you know. And Winston's still a man, for all he's a duke."

Amelia was silent. She hated to be critical but Melody could be so...so flamboyant! The duke was likely to think he was dining with a couple of doxies. It occurred to Amelia that perhaps she should plead a headache and not go down to dinner at all.

But a moment later she asked herself why she should care what he thought! Whatever the reason for his putting up here, he would be on his way to wherever he was going tomorrow, and they would never have to face each other again.

Besides, she was hungry.

EVEN AS THEY DESCENDED the stairs, her appetite was quickened by the savoury odours of roast beef, Yorkshire pudding, and something else she couldn't define. The innkeeper led them into a small private parlour where a fire had been kindled to ward off the evening chills. The table was laid with a clean white cloth and in its centre was a tiny candelabra containing three lighted candles. Candles in wall sconces were also lit, and these, coupled with the warm glow from the fire, made the commonplace room cosy and inviting.

As the duke came forward to greet them, Amelia felt a little tremor. He was so handsome, with his dark deep-set eyes, crisp black hair and chiselled features. Tonight, so impeccably attired in a dark blue dinner jacket, a snow-white cravat at his throat and wearing no jewellery but his signet ring, he was the epitome of understated elegance.

"Your grace." As she made a little curtsy she could not take her eyes from his cleanshaven face, the full lips curving around very white teeth. His smile was warm and the gaze he turned on her so penetrating that she lowered her eyes.

"Lovely," he murmured, still holding her hand.

"Thank you," she said, pleased she had worn the lavender dinner dress. Pleased that Papa had told her not to be afraid of colour, despite her red hair. "Look at the flowers," he had said, "Nothing is so daring as Nature with her colour combinations." Now she felt strangely gratified that she appeared beautiful in this man's eyes.

Melody issued a discreet cough and the duke reluctantly released Amelia's hand and turned to her.

"Miss Harding," he said. "How fortunate to have two such charming ladies join me. Our host, Tribbs, has done his best to tempt us. Come," he said as he pulled out a chair for Amelia.

The innkeeper had certainly done his best, Amelia thought, as one dish after another was passed to her: quail, roast beef, turnips, creamed spinach and numerous other side dishes. Much better than the cold fare they had been offered the previous night at another inn. Dining with a peer made a difference, she thought, as they were served by the innkeeper, his wife and a round-faced girl, evidently recruited for the purpose.

The duke proved to be enjoyable company, amusing them with anecdotes about an Italian opera he had seen and several incidents while horse trading at Newmarket. Amelia was also fascinated by his knowledge of current events and peppered him with questions concerning activities in Parliament. She found she was enjoying herself immensely, though Melody seemed bored. But by the time the sweetmeats were presented and the servants had departed, Melody, who had consumed three glasses of wine, audaciously took over the conversation. "Now ain't this nice," she said, pushing her empty glass towards the duke. "It's been some time since we were together like this, your grace."

"Yes, it has," he answered, refilling her glass and tilting the bottle towards Amelia's.

"No, thank you." Amelia placed her fingers over her glass. "It has been an enjoyable evening, and we do appreciate your kindness."

"Yes indeed," Melody cried. "As I told Amelia, we were monstrous lucky to meet you like this. Though it does put me in a puzzle, sir. This ain't a place where we'd expect to see the likes of you. Now why—"

"Melody!" Amelia was aghast. "You shouldn't ask—"

"Oh, don't get yourself into a pucker, my dear. The duke and I are old friends, ain't we?"

The duke nodded. "It's no secret why I'm here. I have a little business in the area and this is the only inn hereabouts." He shrugged. Then he looked at Amelia. "I admit I was rather surprised to encounter you here, so far from London."

"Oh, you see, sir, it's the most fortunate thing." Melody put down her glass and leaned towards him. "You see, Amelia got this letter and— Oh!" She broke off as she received a kick on the shin.

"Pray don't disturb the duke with our trifling business." Amelia who had delivered the blow, smiled sweetly at Melody who, like Jewel, was apt to overstate the matter of her inheritance. And besides, what business was it of his? She tried to return the conversation to general topics, but in vain.

Melody, her tongue now completely loosened by the wine, seemed bent on keeping their talk personal and reminiscent. She repeatedly referred to "that jolly good time at Finmore's," as if her acquaintance with the duke, which Amelia had divined as slight, had indeed been rather close. Her recollections confirmed Amelia's suspicions that the Finmore house party had been a risqué one.

Acutely embarrassed, Amelia made several attempts to end the evening, murmuring, "We should not detain the duke longer."

"Now, my dear, it would be most rude of us to leave the duke alone with his port after he's given us such a sumptuous meal. Lord, when I think of the cold meat and cheese we had last night." Melody seemed glued to her seat and Amelia hesitated. Should she depart alone and risk leaving Melody to further expose her?

"Surely you are not going to desert me now," said the duke. "We are just becoming acquainted."

Amelia stared at him. *Surely you are not going to desert me now...?* That was what he had said the night at the ball, implying she was seeking his favour. How could she have forgot that disastrous encounter, on the same evening he had flirted so outrageously with Jewel! No, it had been more than flirting. They had given the appearance of having been on intimate terms for some time. Moreover, she had once seen Jewel with him in his curricle. She was suddenly sorry she had accepted his hospitality.

"The hour is late, my lord." Amelia rose and was glad to see that Melody followed suit. At last they could make their escape. "Thank you again for a very delicious dinner, and—"

"Oh, we shan't go yet." Melody's firm hand pushed Amelia back into her chair. "I must tell you about the treasure hunt we had. You remember, your grace." Melody danced over to the other side of the room. "Have you ever gone on a treasure hunt, Amelia?"

Amelia was surprised, but nodded. Here at least was a safe topic. "Oh, yes, we often had such at Madame Suffield's."

"You see, what we did was blindfold all the gentlemen and left them in the parlour." Melody gestured towards one side of the room. "Then all we girls scurried about and hid in the various rooms." Now she retreated to one corner of the room as if in hiding. "We were the treasures, you see, and they were the hunters. Lord, there was many a change of partners that night!"

Appalled, Amelia glanced at the duke, but he only seemed amused. Of course: he would have been an eager participant in that sort of rakish game. Melody was laughing uproariously and Amelia saw that she was quite foxed. She approached her and led her back to the table.

"I think we should all have coffee now," she said. She would have to return Melody to a state of sobriety before she could get her upstairs, Amelia thought.

"Oh, such a good time we had." Melody sat down and fanned herself with one hand. "Poor Eaton had to leave soon after that, you know." She pushed her glass towards the duke. "Maybe I'll try a bit of your port, sir."

"No, Melody," Amelia said quickly. She appealed to the duke, who had also risen. "Coffee, please. I don't think she's feeling quite the thing."

"Of course," he said. "We shall all have a cup." He took the coffee pot from its warming pan and filled three cups.

Amelia resumed her seat and anxiously regarded Melody, who seemed to be rather befuddled and kept saying, "*Such* a change of partners there was that night."

"Drink your coffee," urged Amelia.

"I take it you disapprove, Miss Allen?"

"I beg your pardon?" Amelia looked up to meet his amused gaze.

"I was asking your opinion of such treasure hunts."

"A convenient method of exchange, your grace," she said with hauteur. "That is, if one is desirous of changing partners and has little discrimination."

"Touché!" he said, wincing. Then he smiled at her. "In that case, dear lady, what think you of changing plans?"

"Plans?" Amelia tried to fathom his meaning as she glanced nervously at Melody who was now looking sad and murmuring, "Poor Eaton, fleeing from the hounds like a wounded fox..."

"I was referring to *your* plans," said the duke. "Will your business delay you long here?"

She turned to him, surprised. "Why, no. I expect to complete it on the morrow. And we shall be on our way home the next morning."

"I also expect to finish my business tomorrow. My colours will be in the third heat at Brighton on Friday, and I wondered if you might like to view the race. I have a small place there and can put you up quite comfortably."

Now she *did* fathom his meaning, and her blood began to boil. The setdown she was about to deliver was forestalled by Melody, who seemed to have forgotten her sorrow over Eaton.

"Oh, that will be famous! We must go, Amelia."

"Indeed we shall not go! Our carriage," Amelia said pointedly, looking at Melody, "we must return it as soon as possible."

"Ah, my dear, Lord Chester wouldn't begrudge you a little lark. And you know he said he would not need the carriage."

"That should not present a problem," said the duke. "Chester's carriage could be sent back and you shall continue to Brighton with me. But perhaps it is your own absence, rather than that of the carriage, which would be of concern to Chester?''

So that was it! He thought she was one of Chester's lightskirts!

"Yes, I am persuaded that he will be quite concerned," she said deliberately in a cool voice which successfully masked all the hurt, humiliation and indignation seething within her. "In any case, I would not disappoint him for a tiresome race.''

"So racing does not appeal," said the duke. "Tell me, what does interest you, Miss Allen? A tour of the Continent, perhaps including a visit to the Paris dress salons? And this is the height of the opera season in Italy." He talked smoothly on, mentioning other pleasurable pastimes, and Amelia's fury mounted. She was aware of Melody across the table, winking and nodding, urging her to pluck this plump pigeon. She was aware of the duke, smug and complacent, matching his wealth and rank against that of a mere marquis. As if she were to be auctioned to the highest bidder! She took several deep breaths trying to control her anger as he concluded, "It is surely within my power to provide *some* pleasure that would excite your interest.''

"I fear not, your grace," she said, affecting a yawn. "It has been my experience that no pastime can be truly diverting if shared with a dull companion. Good evening, sir. And thank you again. Come, Melody," Amelia rose, determined to leave, with or without Melody.

"No. Wait." Melody rushed over to stand between Amelia and the door. "Dull company! Lord, she don't know you, your grace! Why he's a great gun—had us laughing the whole time at Finmore's.''

The duke also rose, still smiling complacently. ''I assure you, Miss Allen, that I always endeavour to be an interesting companion.''

''He's a great gun, I assure you, Amelia. Always getting up some game of chance. Remember that shooting match with Lord Hardy? Put out all three candles thirty feet away.'' Melody pointed with her hand. ''Bing, bing, bing! Won the prize. Lucinda, wasn't that her name? Now what do you think of that, Amelia?''

''I think his grace employs unusual methods of choosing partners. And risky ones.'' She looked pointedly at the duke. ''There is always the chance of missing the mark.'' She swept past Melody to reach the door.

But the duke was there before her and placed his hand on the knob.

''Not I,'' he whispered. ''I am an excellent marksman.''

''Your skill nets you nothing if the prize is unwinnable.''

''Ah!'' The duke quirked an eyebrow. ''But how intriguing! I have yet to discover the contest I am unfitted to win.'' He smiled as he opened the door.

''Then I am sorry for you, your grace. This time I am afraid you have neglected to remove your blindfold.'' She slipped quickly past him and ran up the stairs.

CHAPTER SIX

"OH, MY HEAD! My poor head!" Melody tried to sink back upon the pillows. She pushed aside the damp cloth Amelia was attempting to apply to her face. "No, m'dear, no. Just let me rest 'til morning."

"It *is* morning." In truth, it was just the crack of dawn, but Amelia meant to be off before anyone—in particular a certain duke—was about. "Let me help you up. You'll feel more the thing after a bit of breakfast."

Melody grimaced at the mention of food, and it took considerable effort and a deal of coaxing to get her out of bed and dressed before the repast Amelia had ordered was brought in by the chambermaid.

"I can't touch a thing!" Melody protested. "I feel powerful queasy."

"Which is precisely why you must eat something before our journey." Amelia buttered a piece of bread and placed it on Melody's plate. "Just eat slowly and sip your coffee while it's hot. I'm persuaded you'll be better as soon as we are in the open air."

"Well, I can't for the life of me understand why you're in such a rush." Melody voiced her protestations more vehemently as soon as she was fortified by a little food. "The sun ain't hardly up and here we are at breakfast! And in this shabby room instead of that nice private parlour. Really, Amelia, you have to... well, *arrange* these things. If we were to go down at a decent hour I vow the duke would invite us to share with him again. It would just take the merest hint and before you know it he'd be inviting us to join him, just as he did last night." She rattled on about the sumptuous meal, how rich and handsome their host, how lucky the encounter. Amelia marvelled that Melody showed no sense of shame, and indeed seemed to have little recollection of her own abominable behaviour. "Lord, he sure spared nothin' to please us," Melody continued. "He ain't no pinchpenny. Ain't high in the instep, neither!"

Amelia slammed down her fork and stood up. Not high in the instep, indeed! The arrogant, pompous, conceited, despicable... *goat!* Dangling Paris dress shops and Italian operas before her! Pitting his rank and wealth against that of poor Chester as if she were a greedy cat eager to pounce on the biggest fish! She marched over to the bureau and jammed on her hat. Then she paused and thoughtfully adjusted it.

Well, she was glad she had not disabused him of his belief that she was Chester's latest companion. Glad she had given him a monstrous setdown. Though she had not exactly said as much, she hoped he had received the impression that she preferred Chester to him.

"Do come, Melody," she urged.

"Oh, very well, if you insist." Melody rose reluctantly and pulled on her pelisse. "But I do think you are making an error, running off this way without so much as a by your leave. You could pen a note, you know, thanking him kindly and leaving your direction. It don't pay to be too coy in these situations, m'dear. Not when you get a chance like this one. Lord, I'm sure if you gave him the nod, he'd be in your pocket. Plain as a pikestaff from the way he looked at you what he thinks.''

''I care not a whit what he thinks!'' Amelia snatched up her reticule and marched from the room, wondering why she felt a strong inclination to burst into tears.

The groom, who had ascertained the direction to Farsdale, informed Amelia that it was only a two-hour journey. That meant they would arrive hours before the appointed time, but that was certainly preferable to lingering at the inn where they would surely encounter the duke.

He was true to his word, for it was about two hours later that the groom called down to Amelia, ''This is it, I think, ma'am. Farsdale grounds. We should be at the main gate soon.''

They were passing a low stone wall that surrounded a wide expanse of land. Amelia caught her breath at this first sight of her mother's home, and Melody exclaimed over the apparent extent of the property, as they both gazed at the rolling hills and meadows, dotted with trees and foliage. It was another half hour before they were allowed to pass through tall iron gates and proceed along an elm-shaded drive to the manor house, a large rambling structure surrounded by formal gardens.

The door to the house was opened by an elderly butler, who stared at Amelia as if he were seeing a ghost. Amelia, rather bewildered by his silence and his dazed scrutiny, gestured towards the card she had handed him. "I am Miss Allen. I have an appointment at two of the clock with a Mr. Brown. We are early, but might we possibly be allowed to wait here?"

"Oh, yes, miss. The will." The startled butler seemed to recall himself. "This way, please. I do beg your pardon, miss, but the resemblance is remarkable. For a moment, I thought Miss Venetia was come home again."

IT WAS NOT the duke's custom to linger abed. But on this particular morning the direction of his thoughts made it pleasant to do so. With his hands behind his head, he lay, a smile on his lips, a warmth kindling in his heart, an eager anticipation tickling his mind. He did not ponder the cause, but simply savoured this feeling, which he had not experienced for a long while.

Perhaps in his salad days? Not likely, he decided. The youthful extravagances he had indulged in then...the curricle races, boxing mills, the sportings of the flesh...had only been the standard for a young buck of his ilk. He had lost all taste for such capers during the cruel, bitter years of war. And, having once emerged from that horrible nightmare, Society with all its petty concerns seemed more vapid and senseless than ever. The past two years had been dull and empty, and he had wandered aimlessly through them, feeling quite out of step.

But this morning was different: he felt very much alive and eager to begin the day. As soon as Driscol appeared with hot water, the duke sprang out of bed and sent him out again with an invitation to the Misses Allen and Harding to join him for breakfast in the private parlour. Then, happily lathering on shaving soap, he reflected on a pair of green eyes which danced and flashed, yet could turn cold and disdainful in an instant. Amelia Allen was indeed a most intriguing lady. . . .

Good God! He stood quite still, the razor halfway to his face. Surely the mere prospect of acquiring a new ladybird could not have instigated this sudden zest. She was Chester's lightskirt at that—and evidently satisfied with her present status. What was it she had said? "if the prize is unwinnable."

Oh, the devil! When did he ever shrink from a challenge? And with such a prize in the offing. She'd been surprisingly intelligent, though hardly a bluestocking though he had been hard put to answer some of her questions about the procedures of Parliament—when she made those biting comments about the corn laws he could find no fitting response. He was almost relieved when Melody had decided to stage a diversion with her amusing antics.

He chuckled as he laid aside his razor. Miss Allen had appeared quite shocked by her companion's behaviour. Though why she should have been surprised was a puzzle to him. As intimately acquainted as they certainly were, she must have known.

"I'm sorry, your grace," said Driscol who entered the room at this moment. "The ladies have already departed."

"Damn!" The duke threw down his towel.

"However, I have learned that they have not yet quit the inn. They took no baggage and their room is engaged for one more night."

Ah! The duke's happy mood returned. He could conclude the Farsdale business and hurry back. He smiled to himself. Beauty, intelligence and dignity of bearing. That was it—dignity. He could be proud to have her on his arm when he attended an opera or toured the Continent. Yes indeed, Miss Amelia Allen was a woman worth pursuing.

Surely he wouldn't have to remain above an hour at Farsdale. He thought for a moment, trying to recall what duties he was to assume. But the details were hazy. No matter. He would turn all over to Casper.

AMELIA WAS SURPRISED by the warmth of her reception at Farsdale Manor. It appeared that her uncle had not been, as Papa supposed, survived by a wife or children. He had evidently lived here alone, and until the details of his will were revealed, the house was in the care of Tillson, the butler, and Mrs. Grimes, the housekeeper. Both these retainers had known Miss Venetia from childhood and both, remarking upon Amelia's likeness to her mother, treated her with the deference due to a beloved mistress. Tillson had led them into a charming sitting room. Mrs. Grimes, after ordering refreshments for them, suggested they might like to take a turn in the garden while awaiting Mr. Brown.

As Amelia wandered about the grounds where her mother had played as a child, her eyes brimmed with tears as her heart filled with grief, not for the deceased uncle, but for her mother. Venetia, whose lively nature had always been occupied with the present, had hardly mentioned Farsdale. But just being here and having heard Mrs. Grimes's reminiscences seemed to draw Venetia closer, her presence almost as strong as in life.

When they entered the library a little before two, Amelia glanced curiously about and noted that several persons were present. They appeared to be mostly retainers and tenants. Her eyes settled on the man behind the big desk. He was of medium height with a bald pate, and a nose too thin to hold his spectacles. One hand was kept busy pushing the spectacles back in place, while the other arranged the papers on the desk. Amelia's heart thudded anxiously as she surveyed those papers. What did they contain?

A sharp nudge from Melody drew her attention and she turned to see Tillson usher in, of all people, the Duke of Winston! He appeared as surprised as she, but approached them immediately.

"What a delightful coincidence!" he exclaimed, smiling as if delighted to see such dear friends. "How unfortunate that we did not know our business was in the same direction. We could have travelled together."

Amelia stared at him, her mind in such a jumble that she could not utter a word.

Nothing, however, impeded Melody, who beamed at him. "Oh, yes, your grace," she said, laying her hand on his. "The jolliest of coincidences! I vow it must be Fate—as if we were destined to meet again. Ain't that so, Amelia?"

A punctilious clearing of his throat signalled that Mr. Brown was ready to begin. Amelia, thankful for the interruption, gave the duke a curt nod and pulled Melody away to sit beside her on a nearby settee. The duke took a seat on the other side of the room, but his gaze remained fixed on Amelia. She could not feel comfortable and deliberately fixed her own gaze upon the solicitor, who glanced about as if to assure himself that all concerned were present.

"Miss Allen?" he enquired of Amelia, and she nodded.

He then picked up a sheaf of papers, pushed back his spectacles and began to read the Last Will and Testament of Sir Cyrus Fielding. Amelia listened to a long list of bequests, mostly pensions or small allowances to old retainers. Then, with a great deal of astonishment, she heard, "To my niece, Amelia Allen, daughter of my late sister, Venetia, and her husband, Victor Allen, I bequeath the balance of my estate: all capital, investments, properties and income pertaining thereto, including..."

Amelia only half listened to the details of what was to be hers. *Hers!* It was a miracle. This beautiful, charming home that had been her mother's was to be hers. All capital and income thereto... *Papa!* He could rest and get well. She would manage it so that Papa need never have to worry. She felt a great sense of relief, an overwhelming gratitude to the uncle she had never known.

And whom she had refused to mourn, she thought remorsefully. *Perhaps,* she told herself, feeling somewhat ridiculous, *I should don black gloves, just to show some gratitude and respect. To show—*

She sat up as the solicitor's tone altered and she heard the words "to be held in trust for her..."

A cold chill swept through her. Someone else was to manage her inheritance?

"...by His Grace, the Duke of Winston, who shall..."

For a moment she felt utter disbelief. This couldn't be! What did *he* have to do with it? But if her fortune were in his hands...

"...oversee the administration of the entire estate, dispensing to Miss Allen what sums he deems necessary until the event of her marriage, conditional upon such marriage meeting with his consent and approval."

No. This couldn't be true. She tried to stifle her dismay. She had just received...something. Enough to sustain them, at least, and she mustn't be ungrateful.

But she couldn't seem to stop the fury which overcame her! She tried hard to catch her breath as the hot blood rushed to her face and she felt a tremendous pounding in her temples!

Of all the dastardly tricks! To give her a fortune only to snatch it away! *It is still mine,* she thought, struggling to calm herself. But this was abominable.

To have everything she was to receive under the control of that arrogant, pompous, despicable man!

"My! Oh, my!" Melody, who had for the moment been thunderstruck into silence, now whispered her excited exultation. "Who would have thought! Such prodigious good fortune, m'dear. All this! And the duke, too! Thrown right into your lap, so to speak. Now, m'dear, I'll tell you just how to go on."

CHAPTER SEVEN

AT THE WORDS "the balance of my estate to my niece, Amelia Allen," the duke, who was watching Amelia, caught the expressions on her face: surprise, incredulity and yes...overwhelming relief. As if she had just been pulled from the River Tick. Of course with an eccentric father, such as Victor Allen, it could be no wonder that she was in debt. The gossip had it that Victor Allen's pockets were to let and that he had taken an expensive new wife who cared nothing for economies. But if she was under Chester's protection, why would Miss Amelia Allen have a pressing need for money? Too many baubles for even that generous man? Secret debts of her own which she dared not bring to Chester's attention? Perhaps she was a gamester.

"...to be held in trust for her by His Grace, the Duke of Winston..."

What! The duke transferred his startled gaze to the solicitor. Had he heard aright?

At the time the will was executed at that wretched field surgery, his only concern had been for the dying man. Though he had never been pleased that Cyrus had saddled him with a guardianship, he had been prepared to honour the poor devil's last request. He had been glad when Cyrus survived and, truth to tell, happy to be relieved of a tiresome responsibility, or so he had thought. However, though the man had lived, the will had not been changed.

The duke stirred in his chair. He could not say that he did not regret Cyrus's untimely demise. But now his duty did not appear grim in the least.

By gad! What a stroke of luck. With the whole of Miss Amelia Allen's fortune in trust to him, close contact was imperative. There would be plenty of time to beguile... *to win the unwinnable,* he thought, smiling to himself.

Well, damn, he told himself with a guilty flush, the circumstance was providential for her as well. No one would be more trustworthy than he. He did not yet know the extent of her fortune, but he knew she was a woman, a young woman at that, and certainly green in the matter of business. She was deeply concerned about something—some secret debt or vice. Well, he would be most understanding, would urge her to confide in him, to let him help and protect her. He would take care of everything for her. He rose, planning to extend his congratulations and assure her of his dependability.

He found his way blocked by the butler and other servants who surrounded her, evidently pleased that she was to be their new mistress. Then, as they filed out, he moved forward and extended his hand.

"Your pardon, Miss Allen. This is quite a surprise. That is, I did not know of your connection to the late Sir Cyrus. But he was my friend. I had a great respect for him and am as grieved as you must be about his fatal accident.''

''Oh?'' There was more annoyance than grief in her expression and the duke was rather puzzled.

''Yes, he was a fine man and I have a special reason to be grateful to him. He saved my life on the field of battle.''

''Indeed?'' she said without interest.

''Still, we poor mortals have no control over Fate, and, sorry as we both are for this tragic occurrence, I am glad that his fortune has passed into your hands. That was his wish and I congratulate you.''

''Thank you.'' She started to move away, but he moved closer, blocking her retreat.

''It seems that under the circumstances of his will, Miss Allen, you and I are destined to further our acquaintance.''

''A misguided presumption, your grace.'' This time there was no mistaking the icy contempt in her green eyes. ''Let us not place too much emphasis upon a merely financial arrangement.''

''Ah, Miss Allen,'' he pursued in his most coaxing voice, ''surely more than business binds our association. There is your close connection and my erstwhile friendship with Sir Cyrus.'' He noted the disdainful tilt of her nose and hastily added, ''And your father, for I have long admired the works of Victor Allen. I have never met him, but I am pleased to have made the acquaintance of his daughter.''

Her mouth twitched as if she would have liked to disallow the acquaintance, but her good manners prevailed. "Thank you. My father is an exceptional artist."

Encouraged by her obvious pride in her father, he continued on this tack. "I understand Mr. Allen has recently taken a new wife. May I offer my belated congratulations?"

"You may." Her answer, delivered in freezing tones, gave the distinct impression that there was discord in the Allen household and this was the wrong tack to pursue. He was desperately searching his mind for a subject which might thaw the ice when he heard the solicitor again clear his throat.

"Your grace." He bowed obsequiously to the duke.

"Your grace, might you spare me a moment? And Miss Allen—if you would remain for a short time, there are certain details we should discuss."

The duke saw Miss Allen hesitate, saw Miss Harding whisper to her most urgently, saw Miss Allen approach the desk, a daggerlike glint in her eyes.

The solicitor, who seemed not to notice the glint, smiled benignly at her. "Well, Miss Allen, I trust you are satisfied with the outcome?"

"Perhaps more surprised than satisfied," she said through tight lips.

"And so I apprehended you would be. And though somewhat irregular, the provisions of your late uncle's will are fortunate ones for you," he said, as if the words left a bitter taste in his mouth. "This estate, is a modest one—" he pushed back his spectacles and smiled knowingly at the duke "—but it represents, I daresay, something of a change of circumstance for you. I have no doubt that you are most humbly gratified and somewhat overwhelmed at this acquisition of what must appear to you great wealth. But there is not the least need to be at a loss. You are most fortunate that Sir Cyrus wisely left all your affairs in the capable hands of his grace."

"Indeed." Her icy response made the duke wince, but Mr. Brown seemed not to notice.

"Sir Cyrus was of course aware of your, er, situation. But it was his earnest desire that the property be left in control of the Fielding family."

"Oh?" Amelia's nose gave a twitch as her gaze swept over the duke. "Am I to understand that his grace has filial connections with the Fielding family?"

"Oh, no!" The appalled solicitor cast an apologetic look at Winston, who merely grinned.

"Then can you tell me how it came to pass that he is to be saddled with my affairs?"

"Sir Cyrus had a great respect for his grace, and of course you were his only living relative, but, after all, a woman and..."

"Yes, of course!" She tossed her head derisively and the duke marvelled at the way her eyes rolled and flashed all at once. "How could I forget that widely held opinion, as ironclad as it is erroneous, that any man, no matter how blockheaded, is quite qualified to make idiotish blunders in business while a woman, no matter how clever, can never—"

"Really, Amelia," Melody, who had been looking quite aghast, now tugged at her sleeve. "You must not speak so!"

"Indeed, I will say what I please. This is the outside of enough! Even my choice of a husband must be subject to the duke's approval."

"But of course," said Mr. Brown. "Surely you perceive the necessity of that. After all, the property will pass from the duke into the hands of your husband."

She stared at him. "Oh, I see. It is never to be really mine, but is to pass from one man's hands to another's. Tell me, sir, if it must be a man, why was my father not appointed trustee?"

The solicitor coughed and pushed back his glasses. "It is most regrettable, my dear, but you will recall that the Fieldings severed all connections with your father years ago."

"And suppose I never marry? Am I to be forever under the control of his grace?" she said disdainfully.

At that moment, he turned at the sound of Melody's voice.

"Amelia, I beg of you. Please have a care."

As the irrepressible Melody attempted to restrain Amelia, the duke, highly amused by this reversal of roles, was hard put to keep from laughing.

Amelia brushed Melody aside. "Now I see what my diabolical uncle was about. He did not wish to make me a bequest. He only wished to cage me, in place of my mother who refused to be constrained by her tyrannical father. Well, I will not have it so; I will not be under the control of any man."

The solicitor pulled himself up and spoke in lofty tones. "Is it my understanding, Miss Allen, that it is your wish to refuse this bequest?"

Her head jerked up as if she had been struck, her hands clenched into fists and there was a wild desperation in her eyes. The duke thought she resembled a small animal caught in a trap from which there was no release. She took three quick breaths, controlling her defiance, and her voice was firm.

"No. I do not refuse what is legally mine. But it is infamous that it is to be under the control of this...this..." The painful throbbing of her throat was clearly visible as she swallowed the words she would have liked to apply to him. "This...most honorable Duke of Winston."

The duke, moved to quick sympathy by her obvious distress, now spoke. "My dear Miss Allen, do not overset yourself. I am persuaded we will deal well together."

Her flashing green eyes turned on him. "I daresay we will not deal together at all. I know the ways of the ton. You will lift a finger to summon your man of business and I shall have to apply to him, who then will have to apply to you, while I—I— Oh, it is abominable that I am forced to be under such constrictions!" Her voice broke and she fled to the farthest corner of the room.

"Amelia, my dear..." Melody said, but then apparently thinking it imperative to smooth things over, turned and held out her hands.

"Oh, sir...your grace..." She looked from one man to the other. "I...I pray you will not take offence. She hardly knows what she says. So shocked she is, you see. She will come round. I...I..." She hesitated. "I'd best go after her. But never you fear. She will come round," she assured them again as she followed Amelia from the room.

The solicitor, who had taken a handkerchief from his pocket and mopped his brow, now shook his head as he addressed the duke. "You see how it is, your grace. A complete hoyden, just like her mother before her. I warned Sir Cyrus, but he was so set on keeping the property in the family. Then this accident—so unfortunate. Just a few months and everything would have been made right."

"Oh?" The duke, who had been looking after the two women in a brown study, now turned his attention to the solicitor.

"Mr. Fielding was to be married in the autumn and the will would have been changed, you see. That would have been more in keeping," he declared as he began to polish his glasses. "His intended was a most estimable young lady, of the highest respectability."

"A more worthy recipient, I presume."

The solicitor, ignoring the disdain in his voice, looked up. "Well, let us say she would have been more amenable to proper guidance. Of course I would have helped her to—"

"As you have not helped Miss Allen."

"I beg your pardon!"

"She came here with no idea of what she might expect. You gave her no warning, as you should have. You knew the terms of the will."

"But I also knew the circumstances. It should never have been left to her. And so I told Sir Cyrus. You see for yourself, your grace. She is a veritable bohemian like her mother, who defied her most estimable father. Impervious to his demands, she turned her back on all this—'' he spread his hands ''—and attached herself to a man of disreputable character and uncertain means. I attempted to convince Sir Cyrus, in vain, that Miss Venetia's daughter had no right to all this.''

"Indeed," said the duke, no longer able to contain his contempt for this pompous paper scribbler who presumed to approve or disapprove another's right to inherit someone else's property. "'All this,' I apprehend, includes a few horses and perhaps a carriage or two?"

"Oh, most certainly," said Mr. Brown. Momentarily diverted, the solicitor went on to explain that Sir Cyrus's stable was one of the most prestigious in the county. "And, let me see, there is a phaeton, a travelling coach, and—"

"Then why was that travelling coach not sent to convey Miss Allen to Farsdale?"

Mr. Brown hesitated. "I was not certain... that is, I did not know..."

"You knew the carriage was now hers. And you were aware of her uncertain means, of the fact that she might not have had the funds to travel here, or might have been forced to come by stage or mail."

"Perhaps." The solicitor shrugged. "But, as you can see, it appears she managed to travel in style."

"No thanks to you, you miserable cur!" The duke, enraged by the smirk on the lawyer's face, as well as by the bitter knowledge that Amelia had travelled under Chester's protection, let loose a tirade of recriminations. Had the solicitor acted in the proper manner—had he sent a coach to fetch her from London and explained the terms of the will beforehand, then the whole transaction would have been made easy. He paid no heed to Brown's apologies and explanations. "Your behaviour has been most reprehensible," he concluded. "And now, if you please, I'll take the will and other necessary documents."

"Yes, of course." The solicitor smiled a little warily. "I had every intention of conferring with your man of business."

"You shall confer with me."

"Yes, indeed, your grace." The lawyer moved to the desk and picked up some papers. "As you will see, everything is in proper order. I have always kept careful watch over the Fieldings' legal affairs."

"I shall be happy to relieve you of that responsibility," said the duke, "if you will only be so kind as to hand over those papers and relieve *me* of your presence."

The sooner he rid himself of this jackanapes, he told himself, the sooner he might find Miss Amelia Allen and attempt to smooth things over.

MISS AMELIA ALLEN, who had now retreated to another sitting room, was being implored by Melody "not to look a gift horse in the mouth."

"No. I'm not doing that," she protested. "I told them I'd not refuse the bequest. How could I, with Papa so ill?"

"Lord knows it couldn't have been more timely," said Melody.

"Such a surprise. Oh, Melody, I was so pleased." Amelia leaned forward, feeling close to tears. "It is like a present from Mama. Her home, everything she had left is now to be ours, like a gift from heaven."

"Precisely." Melody eyed her severely. "So why did you not simply say 'thank you very much' instead of flying up into the boughs!"

"Oh, you know my wretched temper." Amelia, who was already regretting her deplorable behaviour, stirred uneasily on the sofa. "And I do dislike that man!"

Melody, who was seated beside her, patted her arm. "It's foolish to bite the hand that's going to feed you...especially when you're so hungry," she reminded her.

"Oh, I know it was not at all the thing. So goosish of me."

Melody was inclined to agree, but was of the opinion that the damage was not beyond repair.

"Lord," she said, "I've yet to meet the man who couldn't be wheedled back into good humour."

"But that's just what I deplore! To have to cajole and beg for what is mine. So demeaning. And often unproductive!" She got up suddenly to walk to the window and fiddle with the drapery cord. She was thinking of Madame Suffield's, where in her final year she had handled the bookkeeping and had been privy to the plight of some embarrassed matrons who pleaded for time while they cajoled their husbands into paying the daughter's school fees. She thought of Lady Spooner, who had had to remove her Celia, because, she confided to Amelia in tears, "His lordship will spend money on his hunters but not on his daughter's education."

Amelia tried to explain this to Melody, who had followed her to the window. "And then there was Lady Lucas whose husband couldn't pay because he had gambled their fortune away. And Lady Lucas herself was the heiress—it was *her* money, but she had no control of it."

"Well now, dearie, all that don't signify," said Melody, who was practical to the bone and always intent upon the present. "His grace ain't likely to gamble with your money, not when he's so full of juice himself."

"Oh, but to be subject to his whims!" A noble duke, indeed! He was an unconscionable libertine, quite at home playing fast and loose with a bunch of tarts from the muslin company! And inferring she was cut from the same cloth as they! Amelia jerked angrily at the cord.

"It is unthinkable that my affairs should be entangled with that odious man!" she sputtered through clenched teeth. "I detest him."

"Do have a care, m'dear," Melody cautioned. "One must fly upon the winds of fortune. Best spread your wings instead of clipping them."

"Whatever are you talking about?"

"To speak plain, my dear, if the duke has all the say so, about this fortune of yours, it's best to tickle him with feathers and not scratch him with your claws." She leaned forward as if to intimately confer. "Now, I shall tell you just how to go on."

CHAPTER EIGHT

AMELIA GAZED at Melody in thoughtful contemplation. Reluctantly, she admitted to herself that Melody's words made sense: if she had to deal with the duke it was nonsensical to provoke him, especially with so much at stake.

Her father had been her main consideration from the moment she received the summons from Mr. Brown. And when she found she was the recipient of the whole estate, she had been ecstatic, believing that Farsdale was the perfect place for him to recuperate.

However, there was much else to consider. Would Papa even agree to come to Farsdale? Amelia remembered his reticence when she had showed him the letter, his reluctance to let her go. She had been too excited to realize it then, but of course he was thinking of her mother. During her lifetime he had always been fiercely protective of Venetia and bitterly resentful of the family that had cast her off. It would take some careful persuading to make him accept that which had been denied Venetia.

Amelia pondered this dilemma. Perhaps if she suggested a short visit . . . if she could assure him that his Fitzroy Square residence would be kept open . . . But would there be enough to maintain both?

Oh, how could she have been such a nodcock! Losing her wretched temper before learning the details of the bequest. What was the income? And how much would be allowed to her?

"Oh, Melody, you are so right," she said. "How birdwitted of me to offend them! I shall apologize to Mr. Brown and—"

"It don't signify about that blabbermouth solicitor, m'dear. It's the duke you need to turn up sweet. It's he who has the say so, and it's providential that he has. For I vow he has taken a fancy to you. Ah, m'dear, you shall have him under your thumb if you just heed my advice."

Amelia listened. She had never cajoled a man in her life. On the contrary, she had quite perfected the technique of squelching improper advances, such as those of the dancing master and the riding instructor at Madame Suffield's Academy, and from the gentlemen who frequented her father's London residence. But she was not at all versed in the art of flirtation or coquetry.

But now Amelia, having a quick mind as well as a desperate need, attended avidly to the older woman, absorbing her every word. And so, when at last the duke came into the room, Amelia gave him a tremulous smile, putting out her hands in an appealing gesture. She looked up at him with wide imploring eyes and then, as instructed, lowered them modestly.

"Pray forgive me, your grace," she said in the most beseeching tone she could muster. "I did not mean to be uncivil. It was all so unexpected that I hardly knew what I was about."

"Of course, my dear lady. I quite understand."

She caught the surprise in his voice and risked a quick glance at his face. He was smiling, swallowing the whole. She bent to her task.

"I was unacquainted with my uncle, you see, and had supposed my portion to be small." That much, at least, was true. "Then, finding that the entire estate was to be mine, was carried away by the notion that for the first time in my life, I was to be independent, beholden to no one. Can you understand?"

"Ah, yes. I do understand."

"So, when I discovered that someone else was to have actual control of the estate, I'm afraid I behaved most abominably." She placed one hand to her cheek. "Dear me, I must have more hair than wit to suppose myself capable of managing such things, ninnyhammer that I am!"

"Oh, come now. You mustn't be too hard on yourself." This time she caught a hint of sarcasm and became a little alarmed. But, behind the duke's back, Melody signalled that she was succeeding famously. She gave Amelia a broad wink and made a tickling motion with one hand before she discreetly withdrew.

Amelia pressed bravely on. "I vow I am prodigiously fortunate that my uncle chose you as my trustee. You are a man of the world with a wide knowledge and vast experience in such dealings...estates, er, investments and such. I am persuaded that under your direction my affairs will always be kept in perfect order and—"

"Enough of this fiddle-faddle, Miss Allen! The role of toad eater ill becomes you."

"The role of beggar becomes me even less!" she retorted, piqued by his insight and no longer able to contain her resentment. "Especially when I must beg for what is lawfully mine!"

"That's better," he said, and she looked up to see that he was laughing. "Don't think to hoax me with fluttering lashes and pasty mouthings. I'm too well acquainted with your flashing eyes and stinging tongue!"

"Oh, how can you be so odious! To deliberately provoke me when I was determined to be...to be..."

"Bewitchingly conniving?" he suggested with a twinkle in his eyes.

"Well, yes," she admitted, and found she was also laughing, letting some of the tension drain away. "That is another role for which I am quite unsuited. But," she added, plucking up again, "it is a role often forced upon women, quite unfairly."

"And quite unnecessarily in this case, I promise you. We shall deal extremely well." He spoke with such sincerity that she felt a bit of chagrin. Why should she expect difficulties in dealing with him simply because he was a libertine? That had nothing to do with her—at least not with her business affairs. And she meant to see that their relationship did not go beyond business.

And somewhat to her surprise, business seemed to be the only item on the duke's agenda. He led her back into the library and when she was seated comfortably before the big desk, he sat down behind it and spread papers before her. In a matter-of-fact way, he began to explain the details of her inheritance. As he did so,

Amelia secretly admitted that she was glad of his advice. Her experience in such matters—the bookkeeping at Madame Suffield's and the short management
of her father's household—were as nothing compared to the administration of an estate, the income of
which was derived from the several farms attached to
it. Not only the welfare of her own family, but the
welfare of the families of the tenant farmers de-
pended upon the smooth operation of the property.
Amelia felt the weight of this responsibility and wondered if she were equal to the task.

"All of this need not concern you," he said, as if
sensing her trepidation. "Babcock, the bailiff, appears to have done a good job for the past several
years and I see no reason why you should not continue to retain him. I'll speak to him tomorrow."

"Oh, yes. Thank you."

"Perhaps I should also speak to the head groom
about the stables." He leaned back in his chair and
frowned in contemplation. "Shall you keep the hunters?"

"Hunters?"

"Brown informs me that your uncle's stable is the
envy of the county. It seems that Fielding, a great ad-
vocate of the sport, held several hunting parties during each Season and could seat as many as twenty
guests. Do you ride, Miss Allen?"

"I ride, but I certainly do not hunt. And I don't
think..." She hesitated, biting her lip. Her father did
not care for the sport. But some horses must be kept
for riding. Perhaps Papa could choose which, if he

could be persuaded to come to Farsdale. "I really do not know," she said, suddenly feeling very tired.

"Forgive me, Miss Allen. I am being as boorishly unfeeling as Brown." The duke got up and came round to take both her hands in his. She felt a little tremor in her fingers and stared hard at his signet ring, willing herself not to cling to that strong, gentle grasp. "None of these decisions need be made today," he said.

"No," she breathed. She stood up, reluctantly withdrawing her hands. "And we should return to the inn before nightfall."

"Return to the—" He broke off, giving her an astonished look. "Surely you have instructed the housekeeper to have rooms here prepared for you and Miss Harding!"

"Well, no, I have not," she said. It simply had not occurred to her.

"Then you must do so immediately," he said, reaching for the bell pull.

"But our baggage. We left everything behind."

"You must send someone to fetch it." He turned to ask the butler who entered, "You are—?"

"Tillson, your grace."

"Thank you. Tillson, Miss Allen will take up residence at Farsdale immediately. See that bedchambers are prepared for her and Miss Harding. And please advise Cook that dinner will be at—" He turned to pose this question to Amelia.

"At six o'clock," she answered, trying to decide whether to be angry or grateful for his intervention.

"There are decisions to be made about the household staff also," he continued, as the butler left the room. "But that's entirely within your province, my dear lady. And that too can wait for a few days. After you have rested and looked things over."

Amelia felt that things seemed to be moving rather too quickly. "Oh, my goodness!" she exclaimed, as she thought of something else. "But I must return to London. I travelled in a borrowed chaise, and must not keep it too long."

"Do not concern yourself about that. The return of Chester's carriage may be safely entrusted to his coachman." The personal satisfaction in his voice rather startled her, but when she looked up, he waved his hand in a dismissive gesture. "After all, you now have coaches and horses of your own available to you."

"Yes." That had not occurred to her either. "Things have happened so rapidly that I have not had time to take cognizance of all the pleasures, nor indeed the responsibilities, of my good fortune."

"Quite understandable," he said, smiling down at her. "But there will be time. I must be off to the inn now, but I'll return tomorrow, and every day, until we have satisfactorily settled things. And never fear, dear lady. I intend to lighten your responsibilities and see that you fully enjoy your pleasures." He touched a finger to her cheek and took his leave.

Amelia watched him go, her mind whirling in a jumble of apprehension, anticipation, hope and dread, all of which had nothing to do with Papa, Farsdale or Fortune.

AMELIA SLEPT in the room that had been her mother's and awakened to a medley of country sounds: the crowing of a cock, the singing of birds and the chirping of crickets. She sprang out of bed and threw open the window, revelling in the fresh morning air and trying to absorb this wonderful thing that had happened. "Such a lovely, lovely day!" she cried impulsively.

"Yes, isn't it, miss!"

Amelia, who had not realized she had spoken aloud, turned to see Annie, the little maid who had unpacked her baggage the night before. Annie set down the pitcher of hot water and asked what miss would be wearing this morning. With her cheerful help, Amelia was soon bathed and dressed.

Melody always slept late and Amelia, an early riser, went down alone to the sunny breakfast parlour to feast on wheatcakes served by a footman. Amelia had never before enjoyed such luxury, but somehow felt strangely comfortable in her new surroundings. It was with perfect ease that she asked Mrs. Grimes and Tillson to join her in the withdrawing room to discuss household matters. Both the butler and housekeeper had received pensions, but having been in charge of the manor house for so long, neither could bear to see it run by other hands. To Amelia's relief, both expressed a desire to stay on. Tillson informed her that Sir Cyrus's valet, who had also received a handsome pension, would be leaving as soon as he had helped clear away the master's belongings. The rest of the staff, four in number, had not received pensions and were anxious to retain their jobs. Amelia, uncertain of her own plans as well as of the capacity of her purse, said that at present they must go on as usual.

Soon after breakfast the duke arrived, as carelessly elegant in close-fitting breeches and a well-cut riding jacket as in evening attire. His hair was tousled and his cravat slightly askew, but his alert countenance and spirited dark eyes gave no indication that he had just spent the past two hours on horseback galloping over rough country roads. It was as if a gust of fresh morning air had come in with him, and Amelia caught her breath. She steeled herself against his admiring gaze, but for some reason was glad that her yellow dimity morning dress was crisp and fresh, that her curls were carefully arranged and tied in back with a wide yellow ribbon.

He refused any refreshment, saying he had asked Babcock, the bailiff, to join them at ten o'clock and it was almost that time.

"I want you to be present," he told Amelia, "so that you will know all the particulars and can set your quarterly withdrawals accordingly."

She gave him a quick glance of heartfelt gratitude. She was to determine her own allowance!

However, this turned out to be less easy than expected. When he faced them in the library, Mr. Babcock, a short, stocky man with an open, honest expression, seemed rather embarrassed.

"Begging your pardon, your grace...ma'am," he said in his rough way, first inclining his head to the duke, then to Amelia. "I do not mean any disrespect to Sir Cyrus, who was kind and generous in his way." He hesitated. "But, you might say, somewhat careless. When he come back from the war, it seemed he wanted to wring as much out of life as he could, you see." He cast an apologetic look towards the duke.

"Yes, I do understand," said the duke, and Amelia was surprised by the look of pain in his eyes.

"Well, as things turned out, mayhap he was right." Mr. Babcock sighed. "Be that as it may, it's my duty to tell you how things are." And so he told them, in his stuttering apologetic way. For the last few years Sir Cyrus had devoted himself entirely to pleasure. His parties, the purchase and care of so many fine hunters and his many other extravagances had been to the detriment of the estate. Much needed to be done, Babcock explained, if things were not to go further awry: replacement of a burnt-out barn, new roofs for several cottages, enclosures for certain areas, the draining of two fields.

By the time the bailiff finished, Amelia was looking askance and the duke fervently wishing that he had left the matter to his own man of business. However, when Babcock suggested that they should have a look for themselves, Winston agreed that he and Miss Allen would make arrangements to do so. He had never inspected a farm in his life, but welcomed any plan that would keep Miss Amelia Allen by his side.

He meant to be completely open with her, so when Babcock had departed he laid out some other documents for her inspection. The few investments Sir Cyrus had made were not very lucrative and his generous pension allocations had left his capital sadly depleted.

"Oh, dear. This is not quite as I had thought," Amelia said, and he sensed her disappointment.

"It looks as if there should be an annual income of about three to four thousand pounds," he said. "But of course there will be very little until after the repairs are done and the present expenses are cleared." Amelia chewed on her lower lip and looked at him in obvious distress, and he was convinced he had been right in thinking that for some reason she was in need of cash—possibly to rid herself of Chester. Well, in that case, the duke decided, he would make sure that whatever she needed was available.

"I am sure there will be enough for everything," he said to reassure her. "First we shall see to your own needs. The manor house must be maintained and . . ." He hesitated. "I suppose you might wish to set up your own establishment in London?" He wanted her away from Chester, but not out here in the country, quite out of his own reach.

She gave him a blank look. "But I'm already settled in London with my father. But there are difficulties . . ."

The words "with my father" so surprised and pleased him that he hardly heard her next words. So she was not yet fully under Chester's protection! Well, by gad, he meant to see that she would never be. He had to ask her to repeat herself, but now he listened intently as she explained her father's situation.

Yes, he agreed, Farsdale was the perfect place for her father's recuperation. And of course she should remain in London to keep the Allen residence in order, for yes, there would be quite enough to maintain both houses. Those hunters should fetch a goodly sum, he told her, secretly deciding he would lay out as much blunt of his own as would be needed to carry out her plans.

He made a generous allowance arrangement, and was rewarded by a look of such awe, which bordering so closely on adoration, set up a warm tingling in his blood. It was just small foretaste of what it would be like to have Amelia Allen in his arms, and he resolved at once to exert all his charm to have her there.

"DEAR PAPA . . ." Amelia sat for some time with pen in hand. She had to say just the right thing. "The most wonderful thing has happened. I can hardly believe it myself. Farsdale has been left entirely to me. I cannot help but believe that this is what Mama would have wished—that you should rest and regain your strength in this beautiful, quiet place that was her home. And, Papa, your guidance is sorely needed here. There are so many decisions to be made concerning the running of the estate. . . ."

She paused to stare out of the window. It was perhaps best not to tell him about the duke's trusteeship.

I hope you are feeling much better and that you and Jewel can ready yourselves for a visit by the time I return in about two weeks. Then I shall remain in London to manage the house there, while you sojourn here.

I am sending this letter in the care of Lord Chester's groom, who is returning with his carriage. I also sent a note to Lord Chester, but hope you will add your thanks to mine. His travelling coach was such a heavenly convenience.

Love,
Amy

Amelia helped the valet dispose of Sir Cyrus's things, even pressing upon him the few valuables—watch, fobs and suchlike—leaving her uncle's former suite devoid of all personal belongings, and ready for her father. She made a tour of the house and made certain there were no reminders of Venetia to disturb her father's peace.

However, she was happy to claim one of Venetia's old riding habits, complete with boots, which Mrs. Grimes had unearthed from the attic.

"If you intend to ride about the estate with his grace, you will need it," said the housekeeper. "It should be a perfect fit. I'll just get it cleaned and aired."

It *was* a perfect fit.

"Just as I knew it would be," declared Mrs. Grimes, beaming. "For you're the mirror image of your mama. Now don't go taking them hedges in that headstrong reckless way she always did."

Amelia laughed. She was a good rider and it was good to be on Danny, the bay the duke had chosen for her from the stable. The horse was not too skittish, he had said, but frisky enough to keep pace with his stallion while they made their rounds.

Amelia only half realized that these rounds had become the highlight of her day. She and the duke rode alone, for after the first day, Mr. Babcock left them on their own. Melody, naturally indolent, never rode. Besides, she bent all her efforts to seeing that Amelia and the duke were alone as often as possible.

"That's right, m'dear. Just keep him to yourself," she said with one of her broad winks. "Nothing interferes like a third party when you're trying to pleasure a man around to your way."

It was to no avail that Amelia tried to convince her that it was business, not pleasure, that kept the two together. Now that they understood each other, it was... well, as if they were partners, seeing to the workings of the estate. And now that she knew him better, she had found the duke to be quite amiable, helpful, and yes, even charming. She appreciated the way he had accompanied her through the stables as he discussed with the head groom which horses were to be sold off. Clearly, he was an expert on horseflesh, but he never failed to involve her in any decision pertaining to the estate. He was charming to the tenants also, putting them perfectly at ease. One family had been most relieved to be assured by the duke that their burnt-out barn would have first priority. The wife had looked at him as if he were a god and even brought herself forward enough to offer him a mug of her home-brewed cider.

Evidently the duke was not—Amelia chuckled to herself as she recalled Melody's words—"high in the instep neither." No indeed, he was not, not when he could sit complacently at a kitchen table, exclaiming over country cider and consuming bread and cheese. And then there was the way he spoke to farmer Tyson about the draining of his field, asking the man's opinion of how it should be done, and listening gravely to his reply. Before they left, she could see the farmer was puffed up with pride, having told the duke how they should go about it.

But only unconsciously did Amelia realize her own pleasure in these excursions. The companionship, the joking, even the strange sensations which possessed her each time Winston touched her hand or bent close in consultation—all so gradually became part of her days that she merely absorbed the joy of it.

Amelia's horseback riding had been confined to the little park behind her house and the milktoast jaunts with the girls at the academy. Never until now had she ever galloped wildly down a long stretch of turf, the wind tearing at her hair. And she had not been frightened, but felt utterly safe with the duke riding beside her. He had even coaxed her over a few low hedges, carefully instructing her, "Don't hold back! Give yourself over to the rhythm of the horse."

She was grateful for his instructions, and told him so. They had paused by a stream to share the luncheon Cook had packed for them. It was good: cold chicken, cucumber sandwiches and a tall bottle of wine. Amelia ate heartily and, warm from the heat and the ride, consumed more than her usual portion of wine. She felt in good spirits and smiled happily at the duke, who was seated on the bank beside her.

"I believe I'm becoming quite a horsewoman," she said. "Thank you for the lessons, kind sir."

"Please do not mention it, fair lady. And," he added, a suggestive twinkle lighting his eyes, "if you are very good, I might be persuaded to teach you many things.''

"Such as?''

"Oh, let me see. How to ford a stream or...perhaps handle a phaeton with a team of four.''

"No. No team, thank you.'' She said, laughing and reaching back to retie the ribbon that had slipped from her hair.

"Oh, well then, we'll settle for a pair. Here, let me,'' he said, taking the ribbon from her. "Shall it be a high-perch phaeton?''

"Definitely high-perch,'' she said, joining in the joke. "New and shiny and drawn by a pair of exquisitely matched bays...'' Her voice trailed off as she felt his fingers graze her neck and lift her hair.

"There,'' he said as he retied the ribbon. "And with an exquisitely beautiful lady expertly handling the reins. Would you like that, my sweet?''

"I...I doubt I could become an expert.'' Her voice faltered, her gaze held by the expression in his eyes.

"Ah, but you would be, under my tutelage—expert at so many things.'' His voice was a soft caress as his lips touched hers, ever so lightly, but with such tenderness that within her a hot wave of undiscovered passion leapt in response.

As if sensing her surrender, he kissed her again and again, trailing a path across her cheek, nibbling her earlobe, tracing her mouth with the tip of his tongue. Then his lips were again on hers...now pressing hard...now barely touching...teasing, begging, demanding....

Amelia, who had never been kissed before, drank in the sweetness. Dimly she was aware of the gurgling of the brook, the chirping of a robin, the pungent odour of grass as she was pushed back upon it. Aware, too, of the duke bending over her, whispering, "My beautiful sweet... my little love," aware of his mouth nuzzling her throat, his hand unbuttoning her habit, slipping under her camisole to caress her—

She sat up in a frenzy, giving him such a violent push that he fell backwards. "How dare you!" she sputtered as she sprang to her feet and hastily refastened the buttons.

He, too, stood, looking quite confused. "But you were... That is, I thought..."

In a flash she remembered what he had thought: that she was a plaything to be tossed from one man to another, a woman who permitted... And she had allowed him to kiss her, had been swept away by the wanting, the loving, the... Oh, she was so ashamed— so hurt—so enraged!

She lashed out, defending herself and hurting him in the only way available to her.

"Dear me!" she said, forcing herself to speak without a tremor. "I'm afraid I became quite carried away. I fear I've been too long away from my...my..." She almost choked on the lie, then spat it out defiantly, "My lover!"

CHAPTER NINE

"Now, don't look so cast down, m'dear," Melody admonished as their travelling coach pulled onto the turnpike to take them back to London. "And don't you try to fob me off, neither. It's plain as a pikestaff that you and the duke have had a little set-to, what with him not appearing at all yesterday and you bound to set off as soon as we could get ourselves packed. I vow the best thing that you could do is to meet him in London and put things right. Lord, Amelia, one little tiff don't signify. I can't count the times I had to tease Eaton out of the sullens."

Amelia stared at the passing fields, closing her ears to Melody's voice. But she could not shut out her own thoughts, could not dislodge the shame which swelled like a painful lump in the pit of her stomach. She had been so gullible, completely taken in by his facade of friendship and respect. And then... for a brief moment it all came back to her: the ecstasy, the unexpected yearning and the excruciating delight with which her body had responded to his caresses. As if... *Oh, dear God! There surely must be a bit of the wanton in me!*

"Stop chewing on your lip in that agonizing way! Ain't no use to fret. You can bring him round. When we get settled, just put on your best—that green walking dress, I think, and that chip straw that sets off them red curls of yours to a nicety. You go right round to Ramsay Place. I got his direction from his man, Driscol. Pays to take note of these things, you know."

Oh, the humiliation! *The humiliation!* She had acted like a loose woman. And yes, told him in no uncertain terms that she *was* one! And she was glad she had! She didn't care a fig what he thought! She blinked rapidly, holding back the tears. She had only thought of hurting him as she had been hurt.

"Yes, indeed." Melody nodded complacently. "That green dress . . . just the thing. Now, don't go shaking your head. You must go. It's always up to the woman to make amends. Even if the spat's his fault, a gentleman can't bring himself to come round first. They are so stuck up with pride, you know."

Suddenly Amelia turned a blank gaze on Melody. *Pride.* All she had done was prick his pride with her talk about a nonexistent lover. He couldn't be hurt, for his heart, his feelings were not engaged.

"Now I'll tell you just how to go on. When you get to Ramsay Place, you must—"

"Oh, Melody, do be quiet! I have no intention of going to Ramsay Place!" Nor did she intend to see the duke ever again, she thought. Any necessary business concerning the estate could be transacted through the mail.

AMELIA FOUND THE HOUSE in Fitzroy Square much as she had left it. The dependable Mrs. Stokes was still at the helm; Rita was still practicing her ribald songs and dreaming of her as yet elusive career; and Timothy was still busy with his scrimshaws. All were pleased about the inheritance.

"A devilish good thing, too," was Timothy's cynical remark. "For you weren't likely to make your fortune painting portraits. You're too blasted honest."

"Oh, hush!" Amelia said good-naturedly. "I have quite enough odious squawking from that ill-bred bird of yours."

She found her father looking rather tired and paler than she would have wished. But he was in good spirits and, to her relief, quite amenable to a sojourn at Farsdale, though whether as a result of her letter or Mrs. Stokes's urgings, she did not know.

"Mais oui," he said. "Venetia would have wanted it...that we share what had been hers. Strange that we should be the ones to return. But—" he sighed *"—c'est la vie!"*

It was Jewel who, for some unaccountable reason, delayed their departure. That puzzled Amelia, for she had thought her stepmother would be anxious to remove to Farsdale. And so she had been, according to Mrs. Stokes.

"Spouting off to everyone," said the housekeeper, "all about what an heiress you are. And running off to the modiste, the bootmaker and I don't know what else. As if all the finery she's got ain't good enough for the splash she's going to make when she gets to Farsdale Manor, which in any event ain't the castle she's making it out to be." Mrs. Stokes shook her head. "Carrying on like she'll be rubbing shoulders with dukes and duchesses and even the Prince Regent himself, which ain't at all likely for the nobility's as scarce as hens' teeth in Covington Corners. And the local gentry don't take to loose living, so that one had best mend her manners afore she gets among them.''

At first, she had been anxious to go. Then why, Amelia wondered, was she delaying their departure now? "In a few days," Jewel would say. "There are things I must attend to." And she would be off on another unexplained errand. Amelia would have thought she was meeting with a lover, had not Jewel returned looking as if she had just experienced a living nightmare rather than a delightful liaison.

The reason for her agitation was made apparent the day she cornered Amelia in the privacy of her bedroom. "Amelia, dear, I wonder if…that is, could you possibly lend me a small sum?"

"Well, yes, of course," Amelia said rather hesitantly. She was puzzled, already having settled with her father the matter of their various expenses and knowing that he had already given Jewel her pin money. But she also knew Jewel's extravagance, and if she needed a little extra… Amelia put down her hair brush and turned to her stepmother. "How much do you require?"

"A thousand pounds."

"A thousand pounds!" The shock of it brought Amelia to her feet. "I don't have a thousand pounds."

"But you do. You must have it." Jewel's face held astonished disbelief. "You . . . that is, you said you inherited Farsdale . . . and all those horses and carriages and money. And if you don't let me give him what he wants he will spoil everything."

"Who?"

"Harry. Oh, how could he play me such a das-tardly trick! The money is for him," she said ear-nestly, "for he threatened to go into a decline if I didn't...didn't..." Suddenly, as if she could bear the weight of her anxiety no longer, Jewel sank onto the bed and rocked back and forth, her body racked with convulsive sobs which muffled her spasmodic utter-ings.

Amelia, somewhat baffled and a good deal vexed, took hold of her shoulders and gave her a vigorous shake. "Will you stop snivelling and tell me what all this is about?" But it was some time before, haltingly and between hiccoughs and sobs, Jewel finally di-vulged her dilemma.

It seemed that one of Jewel's lovers, a certain Harry Devonshire, on the brink of debtors' prison, had found a way to share in the good fortune Jewel had babbled so freely about. For a mere one thousand pounds, he would refrain from disgracing Jewel by exposing to the world three love letters she had writ-ten to him.

"How could he do this!" cried Jewel. "Just now, when we are about to be elevated to our proper sta-tion. He will spoil everything! You must not let him. You must give me the money for him, Amelia. You must!"

Amelia stared at her stepmother in some dismay. To her own surprise, she found herself sympathizing with the distraught Jewel, who cared so much what the world thought of her. But Amelia's real concern was for her father. She was determined that nothing should

hurt or even disturb him. For his sake she would protect Jewel; she would seek out this horrible Mr. Devonshire and force him to give her the letters.

"He won't hand them over without the money,"
Jewel declared. "He's quite desperate. He's given me
until Thursday evening, when I must bring the money
to the tavern and—"

Amelia sighed. Such a tangle. Well, the first thing
she would do was get her father safely away.

"You and Papa must leave for Farsdale on the
morrow," she said. When her stepmother began to
protest, Amelia assured her that she would deal with
Devonshire and get the letters.

"Oh, you are so good," Jewel breathed in great relief. "Just give him the money and he will give you..."
The colour rose in her face and her eyes widened in
alarm. "You . . . you won't read them, will you?"

Amelia wondered how she was to know she was
buying the genuine article if she didn't examine it. But
she shook her head, managing to hide her disgust, and
Jewel seemed satisfied.

"Oh, thank you, Amelia. It's so good of you," she
said, beaming at her. "Yes, I'll go now and finish
packing. We'll be off early in the morning. Oh,
my...Farsdale."

THE NEXT MORNING as they were about to depart,
Jewel, still bursting with gratitude, even went as far as
to kiss Amelia's cheek and murmur, "Such a dear,
dear daughter, to take care of everything."

Mrs. Stokes, quite struck by these ministrations,
stared suspiciously after the departing carriage. "Now

what is that one about? Never knew her to play mama before. And what is this 'everything' you're taking care of, missy?''

Amelia only smiled and shrugged. She was wondering just how she was to "take care of everything." She did not have a thousand pounds. Every pound had been carefully budgeted, and anything extra had already been used to pay the bills Jewel had run up. But a man on the brink of debtors' prison could hardly be reasoned with. No, she would have to give him the money.

There was no help for it: much as she hated even to speak to him again, she would have to appeal to the Duke of Winston for an advance on her next allowance.

THE DUKE WAS IN A FOUL MOOD, sunk in the same ill humour that had plagued him ever since he left Farsdale. Of course, it had nothing to do with Miss Amelia Allen—he had known what she was from the start. He started to pour out another glass of wine, but the decanter was empty. *Damn!*

"Driscol!"

"Your grace," the man answered as he immediately appeared.

"Bring me another bottle of Madeira."

Driscol hesitated, looking doubtful. "Your grace, it is a bit early."

"Blast you, I know the time! Bring the damned wine!"

Driscol shrugged and withdrew. The duke stuffed his hands into his pockets and began to pace the floor.

To hell with Miss Amelia Allen! London was full of pretty young wenches.... But not with such amazing green eyes, so full of candour and innocence, and yet so provocatively beguiling...inviting...promising... Not with delicately curved lips that could tighten with disdain, curl with laughter, quiver with desire... Yes, by gad, he had felt it: an unmistakable yielding, so warm and passionate that it had sent his blood boiling, his senses reeling. He had quite lost his head and—

"The Madeira, your grace." Driscol had returned with the wine and was dutifully decanting it, but grumbling. "If you was to ask me, I'd say no good will come of dipping so deep."

"Nobody's asking you, jogglehead! Here, I'll do my own pouring. And I'll dip as much as I please, thank you. So just take your clicking tongue and blasted carcass out of my sight before I throw you out!"

Driscol shook his head, shrugged and took his time leaving.

The duke downed his glass of wine and poured another. He hated to admit it now, but that moment on the bank, by that gurgling stream, he had been possessed, caught in a turmoil of tender passion he had never before experienced. Then...the shock of her words, "too long away from my lover," had stunned him.

Chester. For a moment he was consumed by a bitter taste of jealousy, another sensation he had never before experienced. He had more rank, more money...more... He tugged at his cravat, ran a hand through his hair. Not that he had thought much about it, but ... Well, by gad, his mistresses ... He had certainly given the impression that he was a most satisfying partner.

He grimaced. There must be more to Chester than he had thought. Was she, perhaps, truly in love with him? If so, the girl was destined for a great disappointment, for Chester changed his lightskirts almost as often as he changed gloves. Well, that was no concern of his; he had washed his hands of her. He must remember to summon Casper and turn over all that Farsdale business to him. No need to even see Miss Amelia Allen again.

"Your grace."

The duke turned sharply. "Blockhead! Can you not see I do not wish to be disturbed?"

Driscol coughed. "You have a visitor, your grace."

"I'm not at home to any damned visitor, so you may—"

"A lady. Miss Amelia Allen." There was a knowing smirk on Driscol's face. Not waiting for the duke to speak, he retreated. A moment later he escorted Amelia into the room and withdrew, quietly shutting the door.

She was exquisite. Incredibly lovely. That pert little straw bonnet seemed to give a golden glint to her red curls. And her eyes ... so openly candid, so amazingly beautiful. He felt dizzy, as if he were swimming in their green depths. He blinked, trying to clear his head. The soft folds of her dress fell gently about her slender figure and swayed slightly as she moved towards him. He couldn't bring himself to speak, could only marvel at the grace and dignity of her carriage.

"Your grace." She held a hand out to him, smiling just as if they hadn't parted in anger.

Well, if truth be told, they hadn't parted in anger— it had been far worse than that.

"Miss Allen." Her small hand seemed to scorch him, even through the smooth kid of her glove. "This is so unex— That is, such a pleasant surprise. It is good to see you again."

She dimpled up at him. "I am pleased that you think it good . . . or rather, not too bad of me. It was most urgent that I see you."

"Oh? Well, won't you be seated?" he asked, suddenly remembering his manners. "And may I offer you a glass of Madeira? Or ratafia?"

"No, thank you," she said, declining both the chair and the wine. "I shan't detain you long. An emergency has arisen, you see, and I must trouble you for an advance on my allowance."

"Oh?" She certainly did not waste time with pleasantries. "What kind of emergency?"

"It's of a personal nature and need not concern you. But I must have one thousand pounds immediately."

"I assure you, Miss Allen, that the withdrawal of such a sum at this time greatly concerns me. As I recall, we went over the whole business and discussed your affairs very thoroughly." He had generously increased what should have been an adequate allowance because she said her father was ill. Had that been a hoax? What kind of game was she playing, that she should need such a large sum? And in less than one week! "We decided together what funds you would need," he said.

"I know." She bit her lip. "And indeed, your grace, you have been most understanding. But..." She hesitated. "It's only that something of a totally unexpected nature has occurred and... Please. It's imperative that I have the money," she said anxiously, her desperation apparent.

He frowned. A desperate need of a personal nature. Gaming? That was the only vice that came to mind which could run up such a debt so quickly.

"Have you consulted Chester about this matter?"

"Chester?" There was genuine puzzlement in her face. One might have thought she was not even acquainted with the man.

"Personal needs should be the concern of one's personal friends."

He watched a deep flush stain her cheeks as her green eyes flashed. "How dare you!" she said through clenched teeth. "How dare you insinuate that I would request money from any...any friend!"

He shrugged. "You seem to have no qualms about requesting it from me."

"Oh, but you are quite wrong, your grace." She drew herself up and her eyes widened. "I ask nothing of *you*. I am only requesting a small portion of what is already mine."

CHAPTER TEN

HE HAD GIVEN her the money. Amelia told herself that was all that mattered. He had said he would not have her grovel for what was hers and had written out a draft immediately. The disapproving frown on his face, the set of his lips did not signify.

And she should not feel remorseful. She did not mean to squander the capital as her uncle had, discounting the needs of the tenants and neglecting what was in the best interest of the estate. Perhaps in time she could lower her allowance. Papa would soon be well and it was her fervent hope that before long Timothy, Rita and Melody would no longer be her responsibilities. In any case, this was an emergency. She would take the money to that horrid man, secure the letters and be rid of him.

She had been sworn to secrecy by Jewel, and so did not tell anyone of her mission. She had converted the bank draft into cash and, on Thursday evening, hired a hackney to drive her to the meeting place, an inn called the Sheaf and Keys.

"Here you are, miss," said the coachman, opening the door for her to alight.

Amelia hesitated, clutching the reticule containing the bills close to her and glancing about. She had not expected that it would be in such a disreputable part of the city. The coachman seemed to sense her discomfort.

"Shall I wait for you, miss?" he asked in kindly concern.

"Oh, yes, please," she answered gratefully, and allowed him to help her down. "I shall not be long."

Jewel had sent a note to this Mr. Devonshire, describing Amelia and informing him that she would meet him in Jewel's stead. *But how will I know him,* Amelia wondered. She entered the dingy, crowded taproom and was overwhelmed by the resounding loud voices and raucous laughter. Almost stifled by the heat and a mixture of strange odours, she gave a little cough as she peered anxiously about the room.

She knew him immediately. This was the man she had seen riding in the Park with her stepmother. She stared as he came forward to greet her, struck by the resemblance he had to the Duke of Winston: the same stance, the same dark hair...but not the same address.

"Miss Allen?" the man asked, inclining his head. He was a handsome man and, in his well-cut coat and breeches, was evidently a gentleman, in marked contrast to the other occupants of the room.

"Yes," she answered, glancing about. "Surely there must be somewhere more private..."

"Sorry, my dear," he said as if discerning her thoughts. "I regret that the Sheaf and Keys does not boast a private parlour. But we shall be quite undisturbed over here."

Acutely conscious of the curious glances she was attracting from the men who lounged against the bar, she followed him across the room, murmuring an apology to the fat woman who brushed past her. At a small table in a far corner of the room, he pulled out a chair for her before seating himself, then beckoned to a waiter and ordered two tankards of ale. Amelia, almost overcome by the thick smoke and the foul odour of spirits, wondered why he had chosen such an undesirable place for their meeting. But of course... blackmailing was not good ton, and certainly not to be conducted in places frequented by that select group. Disreputable places were for disreputable business, she thought contemptuously as he took a swallow of ale and smiled at her.

"You have brought the money, my dear," he said as if commenting on the fine weather or the beauty of her gown.

She nodded.

"Under the table, then," he requested, reaching for it.

She shook her head. "I don't buy a pig in a poke, sir."

He clicked his tongue. "Such a suspicious nature! It does not complement your open and extremely lovely countenance, my sweet."

She said nothing, merely looking her disgust. He shrugged, took from his inside coat pocket the folded letters, and laid them on the table. She pushed aside her untouched tankard and observed the packet as best she could by the light of the one candle flickering on the table. Her stepmother's handwriting was on the direction, and, yes, there appeared to be three of them, just as Jewel had said.

She reached but his hand covered them. "First the money."

She handed him the roll of bills and waited while he unobtrusively counted it.

"Precisely as agreed," he said, pocketing the bills. "Thank you, my dear." Then, to her horror, he picked up the letters and returned them to his inside pocket.

"Give me those letters!" she almost screamed until he warned her to lower her voice lest she attract attention to them. Then, more quietly she hissed, "That was the agreement."

"No," he said in his calm conversational tone, "I only agreed not to expose them at present. Surely you would not deny me the pleasure of occasionally re-reading such warm, provocative lines. In any case, my dear, I think it in my best interest to retain them."

The rage rose like bile in her throat, the heat of it burning her face and churning in her stomach. She spat out her contempt: "You miserable dog! Under-handed cheat! Odious contemptible unconscionable blackguard! You—"

"Temper, temper!" he scolded, lifting one finger to caress her cheek. "So unbecoming in a lady, my love," he added, still smiling as she recoiled from his touch. "Well, since our business is concluded..." He rose and began to button his coat.

"You shall not leave until I have those letters!" Her voice was low but menacing and she also rose, wanting to grab at his coat and wrest the letters from him. With an almost imperceptible gesture, he made her suddenly aware of the interested spectators as well as the futility of her situation. Idiot! She had allowed herself to be duped by this miserable man, and as much as she wished to strike that smiling face, she knew nothing could be gained by a public brawl. She had to get away...to think. In helpless fury, she turned and ran from the room.

One of the spectators had watched her flight. He had observed the altercation with particular attention as well as he was able from his seat on the other side of the room. He waited until Devonshire had also left the tavern. Then he returned to Ramsey Place and reported the incident.

"Had the look of a lovers' spat to me, your grace," Driscol informed the Duke of Winston.

HE TOLD HIMSELF it did not matter. But it was like a physical blow, and he could not hide his consternation, his distress, even from Driscol. He was glad when the man went to his own quarters, leaving him alone. Still holding his pen, he stared vacantly at the letter he had been writing.

Amelia Allen and Cousin Harry? No—it was inconceivable, given all that he knew of her. She was a lady in every sense of the— He checked himself. Not quite a lady, according to her own words, but . . . well, different. He thought of Melody Harding and other women of that ilk. In comparison, Amelia stood out like a diamond among lumps of coal. Come to that, almost any lady would be cast in the shade by Amelia. Abruptly, he threw down his pen and walked over to stand before the cold fireplace.

She was indeed rare. And it had nothing to do with her beauty, though God knew that took his breath away. She had about her the air, the innate graciousness of a born lady. It had gained for her the immediate respect, and even the affection, of every servant and tenant at Farsdale. She had a caring nature, as was clearly exhibited in her concern for her father. But she was not stuffy, nor one of those simpering coquettish flirts. Once they had come to an understanding, her manner with him had been easy and engaging. He admitted to himself that those few days with her had been more delightful than any he had ever spent.

And when he had taken her in his arms... The memory brought the blood rushing to his face. The warmth of her lips under his, the sweet yielding, the fire and passion of her instantaneous response must have come from the heart. Or was it merely the expertise of long practice? He gave one of the unlit logs a vicious kick. She had said it herself and with such calm! "Too long away from my lover." He had thought Chester. But now... *Harry?*

He rubbed a fist against his chin. Yes, her flaming beauty would attract Harry. And Harry was well versed in the art of wooing. He would have the skill to ignite the fire and passion latent in Amelia. She would be a toy in his hands and she would never know that she was only one of many.

Guy stuffed his hands into his pockets, feeling a chill engulf him. Miss Amelia Allen might be a puzzle to him, but he knew Harry. He was a reprehensible rogue, though handsome, charming and witty, and as far as the fairer sex was concerned, irresistible!

Women were pawns in Harry's caressing, lecherous, persuasive hands, willingly giving all: virtue, reputation, money....

Money! Surely not...but of course! Harry was a clever manipulator and, as soon as he learned that Amelia had come into a fortune... Ah, yes, he would manufacture an "unexpected emergency." And not necessarily manufactured. Harry was forever in debt to the gullgropers. And of course the compassionate Amelia would come to the rescue! Yes, after the scene Driscol had described it all became so clear! But why the spat? Hadn't the thousand pounds been enough? Or was she demanding something of him...like a wedding ring? Oh, no, she might be an heiress now, but a rather modest one. Harry would be aiming higher. Couldn't she see that he was carefully avoiding being seen with her except in such places as...what was it? Some common tavern. He sighed. He would not have expected Miss Allen to be so gullible.

But... He took a turn about the room and ran a hand through his hair. Whatever Miss Amelia Allen was, she was all woman. With the beauty and passion that would attract Harry. And, damn it, with the compassionate nature that would be easy prey for Harry's skillful exploitation!

Well, he'd soon put a stop to it. He grabbed his hat and strode to the door, then stopped. He wasn't quite up to murder. And a betrayed Harry, all bruised and battered, would only elicit greater compassion.

He threw his hat aside. He had planned not to see her again, but... Yes, it would be best to talk to

Amelia, to apprise her somehow of Harry's diabolical character, though she might not believe him.

Well, there was one thing he *could* do. He went over to his desk and rapidly tore into pieces the letter he had been writing, which summoned Casper to take over the Farsdale business. He'd continue to handle it himself, and as long as he had control of her money, he'd make damn sure that Harry Devonshire did not get another brass farthing!

AMELIA LIVED IN constant fear that Harry Devonshire would demand more money. What other reason had he for retaining the letters? She upbraided herself for being tricked and allowing him to continue to hold them to ransom. Next time . . . but dear God, let there not be a next time!

Since her father's illness, Amelia had greatly curtailed the evening social gatherings at Fitzroy Square. After the departure of Victor and Jewel to Farsdale, these festivities ceased altogether. However, one visitor continued to call almost daily—the affable Marquis of Chester. Often his man appeared at the kitchen door with some bounty for the household: a stringer of fish from his lordship's catch that morning, or a basket of fruit from his country estate. Amelia, appreciative of his many kindnesses and noting that his manner was now that of a respectful friend, treated him as such. All tension between them had disappeared, and she found his company a welcome relief from her mundane household duties and her anxiety about the letters. Particularly welcome was Chester's news that he had once sponsored a man who now headed a touring company and was at present in need of a comic singer. His lordship had arranged an audition for Rita.

IT WAS STILL EARLY in the day when the Duke of Winston alighted from his curricle outside the Allen residence. His ears were at once assaulted by the loud banging of a pianoforte and the sound of a ringing soprano voice. He frowned up at the open window but proceeded to mount the steps and pulled at the knocker. The door was opened by a short man with a wooden leg.

"Shiver me timbers!" croaked the parrot perched on the man's shoulder.

"And the top of the morning to you, old chap!" The duke grinned and lightly stroked the brightly coloured feathers. "Sylvester and I are old friends," he explained to Timothy as he handed over his card. "Is Miss Allen at home?" he asked, all too aware that his eagerness to see her again had little to do with his mission.

"Wait here. I'll see," said Timothy, without so much as a "your grace." He walked a little way down the hall and went through a set of double doors, leaving them slightly ajar so that the volume of the music increased.

The duke shifted his position to get a clear view of the singer, a pretty blond girl who blinked and winked at her unseen audience in such a confidingly humorous way that he found himself laughing at her grimaces even before he caught the lyrics of her ribald song:

"From 'orace's 'ugs and 'is kisses such a thrill do
I get,
But 'orace's pocket is out to let.
I caught the fancy of a bloke whose kisses left me
cold
'Til I learned that 'is pockets was lined with gold.
Dear 'orace, I said, it's time we must part;
There's more to life than a broken heart.
I've a fancy for diamonds and furs keep me
warm.
What good is love 'gainst a cold, wet storm!"

The duke began to laugh as the girl spread her arms
and went into the rollicking chorus:

"Ladiladila, a girl has to live
Ladiladila—"

She stopped abruptly. Then, nodding to whoever
was listening, touched her accompanist on the shoulder and the tinkling sounds of the pianoforte also
ceased. The two musicians moved out of his view,
presumably leaving by another exit. He felt strangely
disappointed. The girl was good, the song funny and
he would have liked to hear the end of it.

An amused smile was still on his face when the man
and the parrot returned and led him through the double doors. Then his smile faded.

The only occupants of the room were Amelia and
Lord Chester, seated quite cosily on the sofa, coffee
and the remains of a repast on the low table before
them. Breakfast? Had the blasted bloke spent the

night here? Suddenly the room seemed much too warm and he was assailed by a series of violent tremors which rolled and pitched inside him, though he was as hard put to explain his fury as he was to restrain it.

The sardonic gleam in Chester's drowsy grey eyes suggested that he was reading his every thought, and Winston returned his cordial greeting through clenched teeth, unable to refrain from adding, "So surprised to see you about at this hour. Isn't it a bit early for morning calls?"

"Oh, Miss Allen and I don't stand on ceremony," Chester replied, looking so smug that Winston wanted to plant him a facer. "Come to that, what brings *you* about so early?"

"Business," the duke lied, telling himself that, damn it, in a way it *was* business!

"Dear me," Chester drawled. "Has the capable Casper quite deserted you?"

"There are some things that a man must see to himself," he said crisply, irritated by this sparring.

"Oh, well, if you've come to arrange to have your likeness taken, you're a bit late. Or early, rather, Allen is away at present and—"

"I am well aware of Allen's absence!" the duke snapped, strongly resenting the man's proprietary air. "And I'll thank you not to—" He stopped, suddenly realizing that Amelia was standing as if to place herself as a barrier between himself and Chester. His greeting to her had been almost perfunctory, so incensed was he by Chester's presence. Now he stared at her. How lovely she looked, and how incredibly innocent, in that stylish morning dress of spanking-white muslin, a tiny sprig of white blossoms tucked in her hair.

"Do have a seat, your grace." She gestured towards a chair. He took the seat but declined refreshment.

"I was hoping to have a private word with you," he said to Amelia, then looked pointedly at Lord Chester.

Chester took a sip of coffee, ignoring the hint.

"Oh?" said Amelia. "Has something gone amiss at Farsdale? Is it Papa?" She looked so worried that he hastened to reassure her.

"No," he said. He glanced at Chester. "It's a personal matter."

Now she looked wary, but her manner was composed as she turned to Chester. "Would you please excuse us, your lordship?" she asked. She hesitated a moment. Then, as if feeling a need to explain, added, "His grace was a friend of my uncle's and was given...that is, has some interest in the matter of my inheritance."

The duke watched surprise register on the other man's face before Chester reluctantly rose and bowed over Amelia's hand. "Then I shall leave you for now, my dear. Unless...perhaps I can be of service?"

Amelia shook her head. "No, thank you, your lordship."

"Then, until tomorrow, my sweet. If you have need of me before then, just send a note." He kissed her hand so possessively before slowly strolling from the room that the duke's blood began to boil.

He turned to vent his rage upon Amelia. "So you did not see fit to inform Lord Chester of my interest in your inheritance?"

"I am not in the habit of bandying about my affairs to the general public."

"General public?" He raised an eyebrow. "Lord Chester gives . . . shall we say, all the appearance of a more intimate acquaintance." He suddenly had an appalling thought: was largesse received from Chester also passed on to Harry?

She regarded him steadily. "You have something to discuss with me, your grace?"

"What? Oh, indeed I have." He stood up and glared down at her. "It's a pity you do not have the same concern about your appearances among the general public."

"Oh?"

"You were seen in a rather disreputable establishment with a man of questionable character."

For a moment he thought he saw a flash of alarm in those green eyes. But she folded her hands in her lap and said quite composedly, "I was not aware that your trusteeship extended to keeping watch on my comings and goings."

"Well, it does extend to your finances! And I demand to know what you did with the thousand pounds you received from me two days ago."

A shadow crossed her face and a flush stained her cheeks. She was silent for a moment, then she looked up at him. "You are a rich man, your grace?"

"Er...yes." He wondered if she had discerned that to avoid depleting her capital, he had advanced the thousand pounds from his own funds.

"And from time to time you draw funds from your holdings for your personal use?"

"Of course."

"Are you required to explain to what use you intend to put these funds?"

"Now, look here," he said, quite exasperated. "This has nothing at all to do with—"

"Please answer the question. Are you required to explain to anyone—anyone at all—whether you intend to use the money to buy a horse, do a bit of gambling or indulge yourself in whatever pleasure or extravagance you wish?"

"No, of course not. But—"

"But, as a woman, I do not have that privilege?"

This was not going at all well. He had put her on the defensive by lashing out at her when he had only meant to warn her about Harry. But something, perhaps the sight of Chester, or just the whole damnable situation, had put him off his mettle. Certainly no woman had ever thrown his emotions into such a mad tangle! In any case, he thought, running a hand distractedly through his hair, how did you tell a woman she was making a damn fool of herself over a worthless rascal—or worse, permitting him to drain away her livelihood?

Forcing himself to remain calm, he sat beside her.

"Miss Allen...Amelia. Please understand. I am acting as a friend. On the day you learned of your inheritance, you told me you were pleased because it made you independent—beholden to no one. Do you remember?"

She nodded, her eyes evading his.

"I wish only to keep that independence for you. I have been completely open with you. If things were to continue as they had been going during the past few years, everything—the whole estate—would soon be lost. I thought you understood that when we decided together how much you could safely withdraw."

Again she nodded.

"A thousand pounds is a great deal of money. Such withdrawals threaten the very independence you desire. Does your unexpected emergency merit such a threat?" He bent towards her in urgent appeal, hoping she would tell him, give him a confidence.

She wanted to tell him. She wanted to lean against that broad shoulder and pour her heart out, to allow someone to share the burden...to help her. But Jewel had sworn her to secrecy and she couldn't expose her—particularly not to the duke who was part of the ton, the cream of Society which Jewel so pathetically wished to impress.

"Was the money for someone else?" he asked, his hand gently covering her folded ones.

"Yes. Oh, yes," she cried, her eyes filling with tears. It was Papa she must protect. Papa, who cared not a whit about scandal or the world's opinion. But he set a great store on love and loyalty, and Amelia knew he would be cut to the quick by the knowledge of Jewel's betrayal. He must never know.

"He's not worth it, you know."

"Oh, but he is." She snatched her hands away and stared at the duke, her eyes blazing. "You don't know him."

"Ah, but I do. His reputation—"

"Do not dare to quote the gossips to me. If you knew him as I do, you would never doubt..." She stopped, struck by his expression. He was not speaking of Papa. He was telling her that Harry Devonshire was worthless. As if she didn't know it! And she couldn't explain, for that would expose Jewel, hurt Papa. Oh, what a ludicrous, impossible coil! She began to laugh convulsively, the tears streaming down her cheeks. She tried to stop, but couldn't.

She rose unsteadily and walked to face the window, away from him. She pressed her fists against her eyes, but she couldn't stop the tears or the laughter.

"Amelia, please. I am sorry. I didn't mean to upset you." The sound of his voice behind her helped stiffen her resolve. She found a handkerchief in her pocket, dabbed at her damp face, took a deep breath and turned to him.

"I'm sorry too, your grace. It's just that...that some things are too painful to discuss. Please forgive me, but I prefer to keep my personal affairs private."

He watched her, acutely conscious of her distress, acutely aware of her attempt to control it, to maintain some semblance of dignity. Perhaps she knew what Harry was, but was helpless against his powerful attraction. He wanted to throttle Harry. He stood silently, fighting the almost irresistible impulse to take

Amelia in his arms, to comfort her. But if she loved Harry that much . . .

"I understand. I'll not press you. Good day, Miss Allen," he said and, to save her further embarrassment, went quickly away.

CHAPTER ELEVEN

SEVERAL WEEKS LATER Amelia received an invitation to Connie Stewart's wedding. In her present mood, Amelia was loath to be out in company, especially among the ton. She would have declined the invitation had it not been for the personal note Connie had slipped in with it.

> Dearest Amelia,
>
> Isn't it wonderful! Our wedding has been moved forward because Edward has been made personal attaché to Lord Arnold in his post as ambassador to Brazil. We are scheduled to sail only a few hours after the wedding feast. I shall try to call in at Fitzroy Square if I can find the time, but things here are in such a flurry you would not credit. The reception may be our only chance to say goodbye. I look forward to seeing you there.
>
> > Your devoted friend always,
> > Connie

Of course she had to go. She was surprised but grateful when Lord Chester offered to escort her. And once again she was appreciative of Papa's careful and extravagant selection of her very fashionable wardrobe. For this occasion she chose the turquoise ball gown of filmy chiffon with its matching shawl. She steadily resisted Melody's efforts to press upon her baubles from her own massive collection, which was likely of paste, but certainly glittering. "You need a bit of sparkle here, something bright there... Oh, no, m'dear, a little is never enough!"

But the only jewels Amelia wore were the small strand of pearls, a legacy from her mother, and the pearl earrings, a gift from her father.

"Exquisite," the marquis murmured when he called for her, his eyes alight with admiration.

"Thank you," Amelia said, feeling a little glow of pride. She wondered if the Duke of Winston would be present and if he would also find her exquisite. She gave her head a little shake, appalled at herself. Why did she keep thinking about that man? She had not seen him for several weeks, not since the day he came to the house to question her about the money. Of course the duke found her attractive; he had made that perfectly clear. But for all his kind concern, he had also made it just as clear that he thought her a mere bit of muslin to be made love to, only to be carelessly tossed away! She discounted the fact that she had helped him on in this belief and tried not to remember her own passionate response to his lovemaking. She took Lord Chester's arm and hoped that she would not see the Duke of Winston at the Stewarts' crush.

And it was a crush. The cathedral was packed for the ceremony and afterwards, the line of carriages in Berkeley Square was endless as people waited their turn to join the throng passing into Stewart House to greet the new bride and groom.

As it turned out, it was he who espied her before she saw him. He was standing with a group—his mother, Lord Linton and Lady Worthington with her daughter, Elise. The group had been purposely drawn together, he knew, because both his mother and Lady Worthington hoped to make a match between him and Elise. He was not altogether bored. Miss Worthington, a bird-witted blonde, was rather engaging in her honest naïveté. She was, possibly as instructed, trying hard to hold his interest, so he made it a point to appear interested.

"Are they not the most adorable married couple!" the young girl babbled, waving her fan. Then she whispered confidentially, "It was a love match, you know."

"Really?" he asked, smiling down at her.

"Oh, yes, she had two other offers, you know. Much better prospects. But she said..." Here Miss Worthington struck a dramatic pose and her eyes misted. "'It is Edward I love, and only Edward I will have.' Isn't that romantic? Are you romantic, your grace?"

"Eh? Oh, well..." He pondered the question, but was saved from answering by an exclamation, as Miss Worthington's attention was drawn in another direction.

"Oh, my, isn't she beautiful? Who is she?"

He followed her gaze, and his heart gave a little jerk at the sight of Amelia standing in the receiving line, even as he heard the duchess answer.

"She is the daughter of Victor Allen. And I wonder that Emma always includes her, in view of her father's scandalous reputation."

"Nonsense, my dear," said Lord Linton. "Allen's a portrait painter. A very good one."

"Oh, do you think so?" asked Lady Worthington. "I was thinking of having Elise's likeness painted and I wonder—"

"I wouldn't consider Allen if I were you." The duchess gave her fan a little shake. "They say his house is always filled with impossible people of the most disreputable character and I feel sure she would not be safe there."

"Nonsense, my dear," Linton said again. "Allen is a gentleman of the highest respectability. He once was part of the French aristocracy; his was one of the families ousted by the Revolution."

The attention of the whole group was arrested by this revelation and even the duchess begged to hear the details of Allen's noble lineage.

Winston hardly listened. He had not taken his eyes from Amelia, standing straight and tall, her head lifted with that graceful dignity that so intrigued him. Since that one visit to Fitzroy Square, he had deliberately stayed away. Not because of Chester, or even Harry. Snatching another man's mistress had always been an easy game for him. It was his own emotions which frightened him: they were so intense, so irrational and so strangely different from what he had ever felt for any other woman. This was a game too dangerous to pursue.

But now...he wanted only to be near her. He quickly excused himself, saying, "Pray forgive me. I must extend my felicitations to the happy couple."

There were two other couples and that damnable Chester between him and Amelia in the receiving line, but he was near enough to see the new bride embrace her and hear her say, "Amelia, dearest, I knew you would come. We owe so much to you. Later, before we leave, we must arrange to talk." The groom bent to kiss her cheek and murmur, "Thank you for everything, Amelia dear," and the duke wondered about the connection.

There was no chance to be near her until the dancing started and he managed to secure her for the second set, a waltz. He held her a little closer than was proper and was silent for a time, simply giving way to the joy of it—the grace and agility with which she followed his steps, the natural way she fitted into his arms, the strange, subdued light in those beautiful eyes that told him she was as glad to be there as he was to hold her. When he did break the silence it was to repeat the same question Miss Worthington had posed to him.

"Are you romantic, Miss Allen?"

"Of course." Those marvellous green eyes twinkled up at him. The lines of worry he had seen in her face when he last saw her were now erased. It was as if she had succumbed to the same happy, magic mood that now gripped him. "Do you not know that all women are romantic?" she quizzed him.

But some, he knew, were only romantically inspired by a diamond or some such trinket. "Perhaps

I should have phrased it differently. Do you believe in love, Amelia?''

Now the eyes opened wide, full of wonder and something close to pleasing in their depths. Her voice was so low that he had to bend to hear her.

''Why do you ask?''

''Because I wondered—'' He broke off as the music ceased, the dance ended and, blast it, Lord Chester approached. He eluded him by skillfully maneuvering her between several couples and through a side door into the garden. Others strolled about the grounds but he was only dimly aware of them. He felt the late afternoon sun warm on his face, heard the hum of bees hovering over the bright blossoms, breathed in the heavy, sweet scent of summer, but was only conscious of the girl who walked close beside him, her hand resting lightly on his arm. He felt a compulsion to draw her closer, to probe the puzzle that was Amelia Allen. Though both of them were aware that their stroll in the garden was a breach of propriety, neither seemed to care, and they sat down on a secluded bench shaded by a huge oak tree and continued the conversation.

''I am given to understand that today's marriage is a true love match,'' he observed.

''Yes, I believe it is,'' she said.

''And that you arranged it.''

''I? Good heavens, no.'' She put her fan on the bench and stepped across the path to break off a sprig of the tiny rambling roses that trailed from a trellis. ''Aren't these lovely?'' she asked, gazing at the crimson blossoms.

"Yes," he answered, but he was gazing at the perfect contours of her face, not at the flowers that rested against her cheek. "The bride and groom seem to feel a depth of gratitude to you."

"Simply for listening," she said as she returned to the bench.

"I should like to hear more," he prompted, hoping to grasp some clue to the real Amelia through the telling.

"Connie and I were both at Madame Suffield's Academy," she said, and told him how the young couple had met when Connie vacationed at Bath, had fallen in love and had pledged themselves immediately. "But Connie's father was in the process of arranging her marriage to a wealthy viscount, and even Edward hesitated, realizing how poorly his prospects compared."

"Miss Stewart, I presume, confided in you?"

She nodded.

"And you merely listened, and nobly refrained from giving any advice?" he queried, quirking an eyebrow.

She laughed. "Truly, I did refrain. I told her she must make her own decision—whether to listen to her heart or to the dictates of the fashionable world."

"I see." He took the blossoms from her and twirled the stem between his fingers. "What would be your feelings in that regard?"

"What do you mean?"

"Would you choose the dictates of the fashionable world or—"

"Oh, I am not hampered by such choices. I am not a part of the fashionable world, you see. So..." She hesitated, as if she had not pondered the question before. "And, I suppose that is all to the good."

"Good?"

"To be free of the dictates of Society. Sometimes I think—" She broke off, and he turned to see Chester approaching.

"Oh, here you are, my dear," said the marquis, as he nodded a greeting to Winston. "Shall we go in, my dear? They are about to go down for the banquet."

Amelia had the look of one just awakened from a dream, but she stood up with alacrity. "Yes, certainly. I did not realize it was time." She looked at Winston, who also stood. "Will you join us, your grace?"

"In a few moments," he said, smiling politely. But as he watched them depart, he felt a sharp stab of pain in his clenched fist. He opened his palm to reveal the crushed remains of the rose sprig and a spot of blood where a thorn had pricked his flesh.

AMELIA WALKED beside Lord Chester, trying to attend to his words, trying to rid herself of the fantasy...for of course it was only a fantasy. But from the moment the duke had taken her into his arms, there had been something about the way he held her, something about the way she had felt... It had been almost comfortably familiar, despite the excited tremors that rippled through her. And when he had spoken of love... Abruptly, she told herself not to be a goose. They had only been talking about Connie and the events leading to this wedding. Still, there had been an undercurrent which suggested something personal, as if...

"Of course you know. You must have guessed," Lord Chester's voice penetrated her thoughts, and Amelia realized he had stopped in a spot quite secluded by shrubbery. She stared blankly at him. *Guessed what?*

"I don't...that is, I'm not sure," she stuttered.

He took both her hands in his. "Oh, my dear, you surely must know how much I care for you and want you." As if in response to what he saw in her face, he quickly added, "For my wife!"

"Your wife!" She could not keep the surprise out of her voice. This man who, during the first two months she had been home, had paraded at least four—well, perhaps they had not all been paramours, but they had all certainly acted very familiarly with him.

He bent towards her. "Now, Miss Allen... Amelia, dear...do not hold it against me that I began on the wrong footing. I did not truly know you then...your virtue, your respectability. I would be most proud if you would do me the honour of becoming my wife."

She had told the duke she was free from the dictates of Society. Yet Lord Chester, because of her "respectability," would be proud to present her as his wife to his fashionable world. How ironic that this proposal should come from a man who himself was of such loose morals! And from a man she did not love.

Still, she was touched, despite herself, and waited for a moment before removing her hands from his.

"Thank you. I am indeed sensitive to the honour you do me. But I am sorry, you are a dear friend, but we should not suit."

"Ah, you do not approve of my style of life. But that would change, I assure you. I would not subject my wife to such scandalous behaviour."

She would have laughed at the very rakish Lord Chester promising to behave himself, if he had not looked so serious.

"I am flattered," she said. "It is just that I do not feel towards you as...as you should deserve as my husband."

"There is someone else?"

"Oh, no," she said, much too quickly.

"Then all is not lost. But I'll say no more now. Shall we go in, my dear?"

The large hall set aside for the bride feast was beautifully decorated for the occasion with banks of flowers, a centrepiece and candles on each table, the whole festooned with white and silver ribbons. Connie looked radiant and Amelia, happy for her, forgot for the moment her nagging worry about the letters and lost herself in the festivities. She enjoyed the repast, laughed at the witty toasts and talked with those at her table. Her glances about the room revealed no sign of the duke. She assumed he had departed and refused to acknowledge the little stir of disappointment she felt.

Just before she slipped away from the feast, Connie whispered to Amelia, "Meet me in my room in half an hour."

Amelia nodded and had started to talk with a group of young ladies she had known at the academy when someone touched her arm, and a man's voice whispered, "I must see you." She turned, and to her horror, stared up into the face of the handsome and diabolical Harry Devonshire. Before she could recover from her alarm, he had politely detached her from her friends and was guiding her down a passageway into a small curtained alcove.

"Oh, don't," she protested as he drew the curtain closed behind them. "This is not at all the thing."

"Of course it is," he said. "These alcoves are for the convenience of lovers who wish to speak privately."

"We are not lovers!" she hissed.

"Which is a pity, my dear. Our last meeting was so brief I had not realized how very beautiful you are."

"And we certainly have nothing to say to each other!"

"On the contrary, we have much to say. I find I am in need of, shall we say, another five hundred pounds."

"Impossible!" she gasped, her disbelief almost overcoming her rage and sudden dismay. "It's scarcely been six weeks since I paid you that immense amount for something which, I must remind you, I did not receive."

"Ah, yes. You must forgive me. I confess it pains me to part with treasures which I cherish."

"And from which you expect to extract a regular stipend? Well, let me inform you that this will not be the case."

"Of course not. And it was to avoid troubling you again so soon that I attempted to increase that last amount at the gaming tables. But, sadly—" he spread his hands "—the cards were against me. I achieved just the opposite. Now, shall we meet on Thursday, at the same place, and same time, or would you prefer that I call at Fitzroy Square?"

"I shall not go to that horrid place—and do not dare to come near my home!"

"Then you shall come to mine. My direction is on this card, which I place next to your heart, my sweet," he said, as he took a card from his pocket and tucked it into the folds of her low-cut bodice.

"Viper!" She almost screamed as she brushed his hand away. She was breathing heavily, and could hardly contain her fury and keep her voice low. "If you expect me to frank your habits, you are under a great misapprehension, Mr. Devonshire. For you shall not receive one more farthing from me."

"Oh, I think I shall," he said quite calmly. "You would not like the sweet lines written by your stepmother to feed the ton's gossipmongers."

"Nor would you!" she said, suddenly seeing a way out. As she had told the duke, she and her family were not of the fashionable world. But Harry Devonshire was. "The gossips would not trouble themselves about the residents of Fitzroy Square," she said. "As far as I am concerned you may publish the letters in the

Times." She saw him colour and knew that she had delivered a palpable hit.

"I see," he said, regarding her for a moment. Then he shrugged. "There is something in what you say. Perhaps it would be best to mail this little packet to Mr. Allen at Farsdale."

"Oh, no!" she cried, feeling her heart lurch alarmingly. "You wouldn't. You couldn't be so cruel."

"Of course not, my angel." His smug smile told her she had revealed her point of weakness. "I know you will not disappoint me. Thursday evening at my establishment, then, my sweet," he said as, ignoring her surprise and shrinking repulsion, he bent and kissed her cheek.

"I beg your pardon. I did not mean to intrude." The Duke of Winston's voice was hard and his eyes blazed as he stood at the entrance to the alcove and observed them.

"Ah, Winston! No intrusion, I assure you." Devonshire said, summoning all the genteel aplomb of a born gentleman caught in the midst of a mild flirtation. "We were just making our farewells. Are you acquainted with Miss Allen?"

"We have met," the duke said crisply.

"Then I leave her in good hands. Until Thursday, my dear," Amelia heard him say as he made a hasty retreat. She stood motionless, trapped in the same helpless fury which had possessed her that night at the inn. Her eyes burned with unshed tears as she struggled with her anger and her fear. Would he do such a thing to Papa? Dear God, could she—

"You left this on the bench," the duke said, handing a dainty fan of enamel work and green feathers to her.

"Thank you," she said, finding it hard to speak.

"I am sorry to have interrupted such a touching scene."

"Oh. You didn't . . . that is, it doesn't matter," she answered, still somewhat in a daze.

"You think not?" The harshness of his voice penetrated her inner turmoil and she looked up at him.

"You have assured me that you are quite free from the dictates of Society. But clandestine meetings at an affair such as this one are not considered quite the thing. When you are among Society, might I suggest that you refrain from such wanton behaviour!"

"You may not!" she stormed. The real culprit was gone and she unleashed her pent-up fury on the man who now looked down at her with such scornful disdain. "No one appointed you as judge and jury of my conduct and I suggest you refrain from assuming that office. Whom I meet and where I meet them are my affair."

"Without doubt," he said coldly and inclined his head. "But I hope you are aware that your reputation as well as your future welfare may suffer irreparable harm if you keep company with persons of questionable character."

Her laugh was brittle. "Perhaps. But surely that danger does not exist when I am among the ton. Pray excuse me, your grace," she said as she swept past him.

LATER, IN CONNIE'S BEDROOM, Amelia found Lady Stewart and two of Connie's cousins all aflutter as they assisted in the last-minute preparations for Connie's departure. Amelia hid her agitation as she joined in the excited laughter and teasing. There was no time for the two friends to be alone, but as she buttoned Connie's dusky-rose travelling dress, the happy bride did manage to whisper to her, "Oh, Amelia, love, you'll soon be as happy as I. For you have received marked attention from three gentlemen this very afternoon. Which shall you choose?"

"None!" she said, and swallowing the turbulent bitterness that threatened to consume her, she smiled. "I promise that, like you, I shall be led by my heart." *And, if ever I do wed,* she promised herself, *it will be to a gentle man, not a gentleman!*

HARRY DEVONSHIRE'S sudden appearance and his new threat to send the letters to her father had severely discomposed her. Messages from Farsdale indicated that he was growing stronger every day and she wanted to ensure that nothing disturbed his recovery. Of course Devonshire would not be eager to send the letters to Farsdale, for that would defeat his own purpose. Still, he was an evil man and might do so out of spite unless she paid him or forestalled him in some way. She felt sick with worry, helpless and frightened.

But even as Lord Chester's coach made its way back to Fitzroy Square, her fear was replaced by mounting anger—and with anger came determination. She would not let Jewel's folly hurt Papa, nor would she allow Harry Devonshire to bleed her of her inheritance. She listened and responded to Chester's repartee with smiling politeness, but her mind was busy planning her strategy.

As soon as she bade Lord Chester good-night, she went in search of Melody and Timothy. She had promised to guard Jewel's secret, but she would not do so at the peril of Papa's disillusionment or her own financial ruin. In any case, Melody and Timothy would not expose Jewel. Amelia knew she would probably have to give Devonshire the money he demanded. But it would be for the last time, for she meant to have the letters in her hand when she did so. This time, when she met the conniving blackguard, she would not, like a ninny, be alone, or expect him to deal fairly with her.

When she called them into the drawing room and imparted the story, she found that neither Melody nor Timothy were appalled, or even surprised, at the predicament Jewel had got herself into.

"Always did think she was queer," Timothy mused, rubbing his pipe against his chin. "There ain't no denying she's a fine looker, but how is it she falls for every bloke who tells her so?"

"Especially if he's quality and has a handsome face," said Melody. "What she ought to be inspecting are his pockets."

"Well, that's not the point," Amelia began.

"That certainly is the point," declared Melody. "What's to be gained from a man with empty pockets? He'll be scheming for you to help fill them. Like this scapegrace Jewel's tangled with, see?"

"Yes, I do see," said Amelia. "He has these three letters and—"

"Addlebrained, that's what she is," declared Timothy. "Don't make sense to write to somebody when they're right in the same town."

"And words on paper don't move a man like close, warm company and a sweet scent," Melody mused. "Besides, you can't unwrite something you've put down with pen and ink."

"Now that *is* the point," Amelia said. "These letters have been written, Harry Devonshire has them and we've got to get them back."

"Right!" Timothy pointed with his pipe. "We'll beat the scoundrel at his own game. We'll steal the bloody letters."

"And how do you plan to do that, paperskull?" Melody rolled her eyes at him. "You ain't no marauding pirate no more."

Timothy declared he'd just catch the scamp some dark night and land him a wisty caster.

"And get picked up by the watch to boot!" Melody retorted. "Anyhow," she scoffed, "do you suppose he carries the letters round on his person? Likely he's got them locked in his safe. And what good are you with a wooden leg? Even if you was clever enough to open the safe, which you ain't, you'd make enough noise climbing through the window to wake the dead."

"Oh, Melody, do be quiet," Amelia begged when she saw her two would-be accomplices about to get into a lively quarrel. "And Timothy, do let's be practical." She managed to get them quiet enough to divulge her plan. "I shall meet him at his quarters this time, not in some public place. If we make sure he is

alone and you two accompany me, we can force him
to give us the letters before we give him the money.''

There followed another lively discussion, with
Timothy suggesting they might just take a pistol and
force the letters from him.

''Dear me, no!'' said Amelia. That was all they
needed—a struggle with a pistol, someone killed.
''That would not be safe. I'll tell him beforehand that
I must have the letters this time. And of course he will
agree, though he probably does not intend to follow
through. Your presence will be a complete surprise and
he will have no choice.''

They planned their procedure very carefully. Amelia was to keep the Thursday evening appointment, at
which time she would seek a delay until she could arrange to procure the money. Amelia had thought a
note might suffice, but Melody demurred, saying,
''The only way to deal with a snake is to charm him.
Like I say, you need to be in close company to entice
a man to your way of thinking. Maybe you ought to
wear one of them low-cut ball gowns . . .''

Amelia protested that she had no intention of trying
to entice Harry Devonshire, and finally it was Timothy who convinced her to keep the appointment.
''Best have a look at his place,'' he advised. ''See if
there are any servants about to upset our play.''

ON THURSDAY EVENING, Timothy drove her to Devonshire's residence in her father's coach. ''Shall I
come in with you?'' he asked.

''Not this time,'' she said. ''Wait here.'' Harry
would not be interested in her, she thought as she

climbed the stairs to his flat. His concern would be the money.

The door was opened by a stoop-shouldered old man. He was not likely to interfere she decided, and from the looks of the unkempt flat, there would be no other servants. She had been right about Harry. He made no affectionate gestures, nor did he even offer her a seat.

"Did you bring it?" he asked eagerly, as soon as the old man disappeared.

She shook her head. "I need time."

Harry frowned. "Time? You got the other immediately."

"And quite depleted my available funds. Jewel substantially exaggerated the amount of my inheritance."

"Oh?" He gazed at her with suspicion but she did not waver. "How much time?"

"Two, possibly three weeks. I'll have to make some transactions."

He hesitated, then seemed to come to a decision. "Two weeks. No longer."

She nodded. "I will do my best." She turned to go, but he grabbed her wrist, holding her fast.

"Do not fail me," he said, "or you'll regret it."

"I keep my word. But this time, do not fail me," she hissed. "This time I must have the letters."

His cunning smile appeared. "Of course," he said, and released her.

She was deep in thought as she descended the stairs. Farsdale was her only source of income, but she knew she could not ask the duke for another advance on her allowance. Besides, whatever capital was available was needed to support the farms. As much as she hated to do it, she would ask him to sell one of the fields. How long would such a transaction take? And could she convince him— She almost lost her balance as she bumped into a man at the foot of the stairs.

"I beg your pardon," he said, catching her arm to support her.

"I am so sorry. All my fault. I was woolgathering," she said before she turned away and stepped into her carriage.

Lewis Humphrey stared thoughtfully after the departing carriage. Only last night he had been privy to a heated discussion between the Duchess of Winston and her son regarding a certain redheaded lady who had drawn so much favour from the duke at the Stewart girl's wedding. He decided not to go on his way to Lord Waxley's residence, which was next door to Harry's. Perhaps, instead, he'd best pay his cousin Winston a visit.

"Your mother's right, Guy," he said a few minutes later to the duke. "Miss Amelia Allen is no lady."

"Oh?" Something in the duke's sharp glance disconcerted Humphrey and he swallowed.

"Well," he said hesitantly, "earlier this evening I was on my way to Waxley's and saw her leaving Harry Devonshire's rooms."

The duke looked down at his glass of wine. "Miss Allen is a lady, though rather unconventional in her habits. She called here on some business with me. Doubtless she had business with Harry."

Lord Humphrey felt inclined to say that any woman who had business with Harry was certainly no lady. But, glancing at the duke's face, he thought it best not to pursue the subject.

CHAPTER TWELVE

JUST BEFORE DAWN a violent thunderstorm erupted, continuing with unabated fury during the early-morning hours. The duke stuffed a loose-fitting shirt into his breeches, rolled up the sleeves and stood for a moment looking out of his upstairs bedroom window. It seemed to him that the roaring cracks of thunder, the sudden sharp streaks of lightning, the heavy downpour that battered the trees and lashed at his windowpane were all a piece with the turbulence within him.

Amelia Allen was nothing to him. Why should thoughts of her continue to nag at him, remarks about her annoy him in the extreme? He had been almost rude to his mother that afternoon after the Stewart girl's wedding when she had accused him of neglecting Elise Worthington.

"She stood alone during two whole sets while you disappeared somewhere with that bit of muslin," she'd said. It was the "bit of muslin" comment that irked him most, and he had rather sharply reminded the duchess of Lord Linton's revelation that Miss Allen was of noble blood.

"Oh, these displaced French people," his mother had replied. "They all claim noble blood."

But Amelia did not claim any such thing. In fact, just the opposite. "I'm not of the fashionable world," she had said. She was merely unconventional, just as he had told Lewis last night.

Still, it had pained him to be reminded of her association with Harry. No good could come of it, but evidently she was deeply enmeshed and unwilling to listen to any criticism. Oh, hell! It was not his business. He went quickly downstairs. Driscol would have his breakfast ready.

He was crossing the hall to the breakfast parlour when the front door knocker sounded.

"I shall see who it is," he called to Driscol. No one but Lewis would call at this hour. But why this morning and in this weather, the duke wondered, when he'd spent the better part of last evening here, wagging his blasted tongue? Possibly escaping from Hilda, he decided, as he flung open the door, letting in a blast of cold, damp air.

To his surprise, the visitor was not his cousin, but Amelia Allen, who stood on the stoop, huddled under a flimsy parasol, fighting to hold it fast against the threatening wind. *What the devil!*

"Come in at once!" he commanded, reaching to help her in and glancing over her shoulder to see her waiting coach, the heavily coated coachman on the box, his hat pulled over his eyes.

"Driscol!" he shouted. When that worthy appeared he instructed him to "Tell Ben to have those horses stabled and get that poor man out of this rain." Then, barely able to contain himself, he glared down at the dishevelled Amelia, who sneezed as she calmly folded her parasol.

"Miss Allen, do you make it a habit to call on gentlemen unescorted at extremely odd hours and in any sort of weather?"

"Why, no, but—" She broke off to sneeze again. Then she pushed back the hood of her black cape and returned his look with one of such innocence that he wanted to box her ears. "It was just that I wanted to catch you before you went out."

"My dear lady, only a fool would venture out in this storm! And I suppose it did not occur to you that a note, properly delivered by a groom, would have 'caught' me just as well?"

"But there wasn't time," she protested.

"No time? Or is it that you are so impervious to propriety that you think it of little consequence to call on me alone at such an early hour?"

"Oh, piffle! I'd like nothing better than not to have to call on you at all!" she retorted, her green eyes flashing. "Do you think it pleases me to have to seek your permission each time I am in need of money that belongs to me?"

"Aha! Another unexpected emergency, I presume," he said with sarcasm, his anger mounting. A visit with Harry last evening...then a request for money this morning? The first bundle had likely been swallowed at the gaming table and the blackguard was pulling at her pockets again! He'd like to collar the wretch and choke the life from him!

"Well...that is..." She hesitated, as if she were trying to avoid any vexatious words. "I shouldn't like to quarrel with you. I'd like...that is, I must discuss—'' She broke off with a violent sneeze, took a handkerchief from her reticule and blew her nose.

As she murmured an apology, he noted the dark circles under her eyes, the damp tendrils of hair clinging to her pale face, and all thoughts of Harry vanished in his concern for her. She was shivering with the cold. Out in this damnable weather she could contract an inflammation of the lungs and die. Panic seized him at the thought. He wanted to shake her...or take her in his arms.

''We'd best have our discussion over breakfast as I'm sure you haven't had any and are in need of a good sustaining meal. The fire will warm and dry you,'' he said rather stiffly, taking her dripping parasol and depositing it in the stand. ''Let me have your cloak.'' He did not heed her protestations, but removed the cape from her shoulders and handed it to Driscol, who had returned from his errand. ''Dry this out and set another place for Miss Allen.''

''Nothing for me, thank you,'' Amelia said when he led her to the table and seated her in the chair nearest the fire. ''Contrary to your assumption, I have had my breakfast.''

''Well, I haven't,'' said the duke as he seated himself. ''And you'd better have a cup of hot coffee.'' He waited until Driscol had served them and disappeared before he spoke again. ''Now, this discussion. I apprehend it is urgent?'' he asked, not looking at her as he buttered a piece of bread.

''Yes, it is rather. I need...that is, I am rather pressed for a sum of money and...oh, you needn't look at me like that. I am well aware of my financial status and wouldn't dream of asking for another advance."

"Good," he muttered, refilling her cup.

"Thank you." She took a sip of the hot brew, put her cup down, sniffed and touched her tiny lace kerchief to her nose. Then she raised her eyes to his. "It is for that reason that I am suggesting...that is, requesting...that you sell off one of the fields. As quickly as you can, if you please."

"Requesting? Or demanding?"

She stiffened. "Well, after all it *is* my property."

"Ah, yes. So it comes to that," he said as he cut into a slice of ham. "Drink your coffee."

Obediently, she sipped it, watching for a while in silence as he ate his breakfast. Then, impatiently she asked, "How long would it take?"

"Forever, I fear," he said as he laid aside his napkin and pushed back his chair.

"Oh, you can't mean that. I must have five hundred pounds within two weeks." In her agitation, she stood and moved towards the fire. Then she turned to face him. "That's why I came to see you at once. Surely you can arrange it."

"I think not." He got up, stuck his hands into his pockets and looked solemnly down at her. "I am obliged to tell you that only one of your tenants would desire to purchase one field. And none could afford that purchase price."

"Oh," she said, placing her hand on the mantel as if for support. "Then we must sell one of the farms."

He shook his head. "Impossible." He did not intend to let Harry bleed her dry.

"Why impossible? The farms are mine. You have no right to keep me from selling one."

"Ah, but I do have that right."

"Oh, fiddle! Why on earth should you care? I tell you—" She stopped to dab at her nose with the now useless handkerchief.

"Take this," he said, providing his own crisp monogrammed linen square.

"Thank you." Gratefully she blew into it, returning hers to her pocket. "Your grace, I do not like to trouble you, but..." She hesitated, twisting the white square in her hands. "It's imperative that I acquire the money. I shall not ask for an advance again. I promise."

He swallowed a lump in his throat as he watched her. Not the confident lady in the chic straw hat that had so beguiled him the first time she had come for funds. This time she looked distraught, bedraggled; her eyes were swollen, her nose red and running. And he had never cared so deeply for any woman. Not ever.

"Amelia," he said huskily, a wave of tenderness sweeping through him. "Tell me. Why this pressing need?" Perhaps if she would confide in him, he could dissuade her.

She shook her head. "I... I'd rather not say your grace."

Gently he brushed a damp lock of hair from her forehead. "Do you not trust me?"

"It is not that. Please. I am not at liberty to... That is, it involves someone else."

Of course. He knew that. He looked down at her fingers, now desperately clutching his handkerchief. It pained him to see her with so little regard for her pride, pleading for Harry who didn't deserve her.

"Stop this!" he said sharply, covering her hands with his. "I can't bear to see you in such a state."

She smiled tremulously, blinking through sudden tears. "I'm sorry. I didn't mean to be so...so persistent. It's just that I need to...to... Please. If I don't acquire the money someone may be dreadfully hurt. Someone close to me."

The distress, the compassion in her voice tore at him. And vexed him. Didn't she know that such selfless devotion was wasted on a man like Harry? He grasped her arms, intent upon shaking some sense into her. Her sharp cry of pain startled him and his grip loosened to a gentle caress.

"Oh, my dearest, I'd never hurt you." The touch of her soft skin through the thin muslin of her gown sent such a surge of passion flooding through his veins that his arms slipped round her. He held her close and whispered in her ear, "I only want to help. I want you to be happy." She would be happy. He would see to that. He stared down at her, tracing with his eyes the delicate contours of her lovely face, the delicate curve of her slender neck, the silken tresses so brilliant against her pale skin. And he saw the apprehension which lurked behind the hope in those dazzling green eyes, the fear throbbing so painfully in the pulse at the base of her throat.

"Put your trust in me," he urged in answer to the unspoken question in her wary eyes, even as he touched his lips to her throat as if to quiet the leaping pulse there. Intoxicated by the sweet scent of her, he nuzzled closer, trailing light kisses along her neck and across her cheek. "Ah, my sweet," he murmured in her ear, "Let me love and protect you. I shall love you as you have never been loved. I shall shield you from every pain, every storm." He nibbled at her earlobe, heard her sigh of pleasure and raised his head to see her lips parted in invitation as she pressed closer to him in unmistakable surrender. His emotions bounced and skittered in a mad jumble, his joyous confidence mounting to a peak which matched the strength of the storm that roared and thundered outside his window.

She heard the sound of rain lashing at the windows, the whistling of the wind and the distant roar of thunder, but they had nothing to do with her. Enfolded in his strong arms she felt warm and safe, wrapped in a silken cocoon where nothing could harm her. Harry, the letters, all problems were forgotten. She felt blissfully happy, fully alive. He loved her! When his lips possessed hers, she quivered with excitement, engulfed in a whirlwind of passion and responded with every fibre of her being.

"Ah, my love, what a delight you are," he whispered, his lips lingering on hers as if he could not bear to part from them. "We shall be so happy, all alone in our little love nest. You'll see. Under my protection you'll never want for anything."

Slowly, inexorably, his words penetrated her euphoric daze. "Love nest...under my protection." She stiffened. How could she forget?

Oh, what an idiotish fool she was! His love was not real. He did not mean... He only wanted her for a plaything...a bit of muslin. Her face burned with disappointment, with humiliation.

He twisted one of her curls about his finger as he continued to whisper in her ear. She had long since ceased to listen but her attention was caught by the words "I'll find a place where we can be alone, just the two of us, and—" He broke off as she pushed violently against him and delivered a stinging blow to his cheek.

"Amelia! Why...what is wrong?" he asked in genuine astonishment. What the devil was wrong with the girl? One moment she was hot with passion and the next... He moved towards her, opening his arms.

She stepped back, glaring at him. "Under your protection! In a love nest! Keep your hands off me! What do you mean, making such a suggestion?"

"We both know what you are, my lady," he said in scathing tones, his own anger now fully aroused. Did she think him a fool? "It merely saddens me that you value yourself so cheaply. If you must sell yourself, it should be to the highest bidder. Harry has no money, and I have a bit more than Chester, so—"

"How dare you! It is not myself, but a *farm* I wish to sell!"

"To support the vices of the man you love!"

"What?" Her look of feigned astonishment was so real that he almost laughed.

"Oh, yes, my dear, not only were you seen in that tavern just after your other 'sudden emergency,' but last night you were seen again, leaving his quarters.

This morning—'' he spread his hands significantly ''—you have another 'sudden emergency.' ''

"You had me followed!"

"And why should I not?"

"How abominable! Having me followed like a common criminal and to suppose that I—'' She broke off, wrinkling her nose with contempt. "Well, let me inform you, your grace, that from this moment on you need not concern yourself with my affairs. I shall write to my father to seek a buyer for one of the farms and if he finds one—''

"It is of no consequence. I will not permit the sale. I will not allow you to make a fool of yourself."

"I don't see why not. Men are always permitted to make fools of themselves!"

That, at least, was true, he thought, as he touched his burning cheek. He could have sworn that she had responded. He had felt her lips quiver and ...

"Oh, this is the outside of enough!" she said, now in a towering rage. "I inherit an estate, but every farthing is controlled by you. Even my movements are monitored. It is because you are a conceited, arrogant and pompous fool, like most men of my acquaintance."

"Oh?" He lifted an eyebrow. "And what do you propose to do about it?"

"I shall earn my own living," she said with calm deliberation. "Men do. And I daresay I have a lot more talent than the average paperskull."

"I daresay you do," the duke answered, a suggestive twinkle in his eye.

Amelia tilted her nose. "I shall ignore your in-nuendoes, your grace. It just so happens that I am a talented portrait painter. I may not be up to my father's mark, but even he says I have the touch of an artist."

"How intriguing! Would you care to put your touch to me?"

"What?" Her eyes widened with suspicion.

"I'll sit for you," he said, a plan slowly forming in his mind.

"You will?" Her incredulity was apparent.

"And if I'm satisfied with the result, I'll pay the sum you ask."

"Why?"

He shrugged. "I am in need of a portrait. You are in need of the money." He watched her expression as she wrestled between doubt and hope.

"I must have the money in two weeks. You'd have to sit every day," she said.

"Of course." That should give him time: time to convince her that she was too good for Harry, time to show her that life could be more satisfying . . . and in-finitely more exciting.

THE STORM HAD SUBSIDED a bit, but there was still a steady rain when she left the duke's house and there was no chance to exchange a word with Timothy as he helped her into the carriage. It was not until she was in the drawing room at Fitzroy Square alone with both Timothy and Melody that she was able to reveal the outcome of her visit.

"Did you get the money?" Melody asked.

"Oh, no, of course not," Amelia said, still smarting from the interview. "Not even after I suggested a good plan—to simply sell one of the farms. He is the most dogmatic, odious, contemptible man I know. And he is convinced that I am untalented and incompetent, too. I saw that smug, disbelieving glint in his eyes. Well, I shall teach him the lesson he so richly deserves."

"How?" Melody asked as they both stared at her.

"He has engaged me to paint his portrait," she answered and told of the agreement.

"Payment upon satisfaction, eh?" Timothy asked. When she nodded he shook his head dubiously. "It's a fact that you paint what you see, Miss Amelia. And the way you see him . . . Well, he ain't likely to be satisfied."

HE SEEMED OUT OF PLACE in her father's attic studio, his tall, muscular stature dominating the room. His essence permeated the whole place and the strong sense of vitality, the lingering scent of fresh air and sunshine on leather made her feel that he brought the outdoors inside with him. She felt strangely exhilarated in his presence and each morning awaited his arrival with an eagerness she tried to deny.

He was not a good sitter. He would jump up on impulse and stalk about the room, examining everything, probing and questioning as if he sought something beyond the pots of paint and the sketches and paintings scattered about. She did not allow him to view the likeness she was making of him, but he seemed fascinated by her other works, like the one she had done of Timothy with a bandanna round his head and a patch over one eye, the very image of the pirate she always fancied he must have been. He lingered a long time over several sketches of Rita which leaned against one wall.

"This is the girl who was singing the morning I visited you," he said, picking up one of the sketches to examine it more closely.

"Yes, that's Rita," said Amelia, but it was his countenance she studied and rapidly reproduced on her pad. She had no time to waste, and had formed the habit of catching on paper the various moods reflected on his face as he roamed the studio. "She was practicing for an audition that morning."

"Audition? Did she get the part?"

"Oh, yes." Amelia blew on her pad to remove the excess charcoal. "She's leaving with a touring company at the end of the week. She will use those sketches to advertise her appearances."

"An excellent idea. You've caught that comic expression of hers. You are a very good artist."

"Thank you, kind sir. Now you've had a good stretch. Will you sit down and resume your pose?"

He obediently returned to his chair, but, as always, seemed to forget the pose. She made him cross his legs just so, and went over to tilt his head at the right angle and rumple his hair just a wee bit. They were professional gestures only, she told herself, and tried to ignore the way her fingertips burned with an almost irresistible longing to caress his face. And had she imagined it, she wondered as she returned to the canvas, or was there a mockingly suggestive twinkle in his eyes?

"I'm not surprised that Rita has found a place. Her performance was good."

"Yes. Don't move!"

"Oh. Sorry. I quite liked that song she was singing about someone's kisses giving her a thrill and another chap's leaving her cold."

"Yes, that was amusing."

"But not without merit. You see—"

"Don't! No, not that way! Oh, piffle!" She went over to tilt his head again. "Now, do not move!"

"Yes, of course. I beg pardon. But that song is simply suggesting that a girl has to be practical. Remember what we talked about at the Stewart wedding?"

"Hold still!"

"I shall, I promise. You said you had no care for Society and would do as you please where your heart was concerned. But there is a practical side to be considered.

Amelia smiled as she worked and listened to the lecture he always came back to. She smiled because she knew exactly what he was about: he was trying to warn her off Harry Devonshire. The duke had somehow arrived at the conclusion that that despicable villain had captured her heart! Ha! If he only knew!

Of course, she couldn't enlighten him even had she wished to. And she didn't wish to because there was some perverse satisfaction in allowing this confident, titled and wealthy man who had the world at his fingertips to think he could be bested by such a rogue.

Also, she did not wish the duke to know the only kisses that had ever stirred her were his. She was even less eager to admit that though she was two and twenty, the only kisses she had ever *received* were his. For the clumsy attempts of the dancing master at Madame Suffield's Academy surely did not count, since she had dodged them successfully.

But perhaps she should not think so unkindly of the dancing master, for he, at least, had asked for her hand in marriage. Though she hadn't dodged the duke's kisses, he evidently had something else entirely in mind.

She knew exactly what he was doing when he reverted to other subjects, like travel: he was casting out lures. "You are such an excellent artist," he would say, "you really ought to visit the Paris museums," or "You must see the Sistine Chapel in Rome!" He had even said it outright one day. "You could have such an exciting life with me."

"Yes," she had retorted. "Playing blind man's buff at some secluded country estate with a lot of men who dare to call themselves gentlemen!"

"I must protest. I have nothing such as that in mind. I mean to give you only the best, discreetly and privately."

"Ah, yes. All alone," she said, holding her brush up as if in contemplation. For she also took a perverse satisfaction in leading him on, as if she might really consider such an arrangement. What a setdown it would be when she told him he was the last man on earth she would choose to be alone with!

Meanwhile, she almost unconsciously absorbed the joy of being alone with him in the cosy little attic room. Occasionally, they were interrupted by Mrs. Stokes who came to enquire about a household matter, or Rita wanting her opinion on a costume, or Timothy bringing in the paint she had requested. But mostly it was just the two of them.

So the cat-and-mouse game continued, he making subtle advances and she teasing, laughing, leading him on. And the work went on, too—rapidly, because there was the need to finish the portrait so she could pay off and be rid of Harry Devonshire. If she found satisfaction in capturing the duke's likeness on canvas, she refused to notice it.

One day after the duke had departed, Amelia looked at the canvas and made one last stroke with her brush. The portrait was finished. All that remained was to sign her name. But when she picked up the brush to do so, it felt heavy in her hand, weighed down by a strange reluctance.

CHAPTER THIRTEEN

"WELL, I'LL BE. You've done it right this time, missy!" Timothy said, looking over her shoulder at the duke's portrait.

"Oh, do you really think so?" Amelia, pleased, turned on her stool to look up at him.

"Yes indeed. He'll pay any price you ask." He nodded with satisfaction as he pointed with his pipe. "It's as if you put your heart right there on that canvas."

Timothy's words rang in her ears long after he had clomped downstairs. She had decided to try to capture the duke's likeness as he had appeared so many times at Farsdale—his riding coat open, his cravat askew, the sun streaking across his face and his hair tousled as if by the wind. Remembering their many clashes and her tendency to display her feelings in her work, she had determined not to portray him as dictatorial, tyrannical...or as a libertine. But was her heart on the canvas despite herself?

She stared at the portrait. Yes, there it was, in that teasing twinkle in his eyes, in the firm, honest lift of his chin, in the generous curve of his lips—the lips that she longed to have pressed to hers again.

She loved him!

Dear God, that was why she had welcomed his improper advances—yes, welcomed them! She had told herself she was leading him on for a most severe setdown, and she had slapped him when he kissed her. But now she could not deny the treacherous response of her whole body. She had revelled in any slight caress—when his hand brushed hers, or he teasingly tweaked a curl or touched a finger to her cheek.

Oh, she was a wanton! She had pretended to play a game. But there had been such joy in thoughts of travelling with him through France and Italy, cruising through the Greek isles. And when he asked, "Could you bear to be shut up with me in a travelling coach for several weeks?" she had felt the unmistakable stirring of a strange passion that cut short her breath and made her heart beat faster. And everything she had felt had been revealed in her face! She could tell, because his eyes had gleamed with triumph . . . and with something else, something so warm and welcoming that she knew she would go with him to the ends of the earth!

Oh, what was she thinking of! She stood up abruptly and put down her brush. She might not be of the fashionable world, but she had promised her mother she would always be a lady. She would not be trapped by her heart into the stealth and misery of illicit love!

But as she went slowly downstairs, she felt the danger. If the duke continued to look at her as he did, if he persisted . . . and he would persist. But she would not be persuaded! Yet, even as she formed that firm resolve, she felt the wild beating of her wayward heart, and her mind searched frantically for an escape from the danger.

"I was just coming to fetch you," said Timothy when she reached the bottom step. "Lord Chester is here to see you."

Chester was sitting on the sofa, but he rose to take her hand. "My dear, I had almost given up hope. Each day that I've come you've not been 'in' to visitors."

She smiled. "I'm sorry. I was working, and rather in a hurry to finish a portrait."

"You?" He looked surprised. "I thought your father was the artist."

"Yes. And of course I'm not as good as Papa. But this...person agreed to sit for me and I needed the money," she said, rather proud that she was earning something from her talents even if it were just once.

"My dear, if you were in need of funds..." He stopped, noting the expression on her face. "No, of course you would not ask but..." He seemed puzzled. "Jewel gave me to understand that you were quite an heiress."

"Jewel exaggerates. And, to own the truth, everything is in the hands of a trustee and I am obliged to apply to him for all my needs."

"I see. You do not like that, I daresay."

"I'm afraid I can do nothing about it. Come, sit down and tell me—how was your hunting trip?"

He sat with her on the settee, but would not be diverted from his topic. "You wish to be completely independent, would you not?"

"Yes, but I am independent...to some extent." She said hesitantly, thinking of the duke, wondering if he would be forever in her thoughts. Of course, she had to apply to him, and whenever he was near... She drew a quick breath, feeling a quiver of excitement. Oh, dear heavens, would she always be so vulnerable? She tried to think logically, calmly. She was not a green girl controlled by idiotish emotions. And once she was rid of Harry Devonshire, there would be less need to consult Winston. If only he would not persist. If only—

"You could be, you know. As my wife..."

Automatically she shook her head, trying to attend to what Chester had said.

"Wait. Hear me out." Again he took her hand. "As my wife, everything I have would be yours."

"Please..." She did not want to embarrass him by another refusal. He was so kind, so generous.

"No, my dear, only listen. If you marry me I shall make you independent. I shall have drawn up a marriage settlement ensuring that your own estate will be entirely under your jurisdiction and you need apply to no one, not even me, to do with it whatever you wish." He leaned towards her. "Do you see, my dear? No one could influence you. You would be in control of your own destiny."

She looked at him. To be in control of her own destiny, she must have control of her emotions, in particular those reckless emotions which arose whenever the Duke of Winston was nearby. Once married, she would control them, for she could never be an un-

faithful wife. Unmarried, she could so easily succumb to passion and become a fallen woman.

And marriage would certainly distance her from the
duke. Even her business affairs would be transferred
to her husband, or, as Chester promised, to herself.
She drew a deep breath.

"Lord Chester..." She hesitated. "I am fond of
you. I respect you. But...I do not love you."

"Perhaps that will come in time," he said eagerly.
"I am willing to wait."

It was not what she had planned, but it was a way
out of a dangerous coil. She would be a good wife; she
would try to make him happy.

"If you wish it," she said slowly and deliberately.

He was overjoyed. "I shall write your father immediately."

"Yes," she said, and added, almost as an afterthought, "you must also seek permission from another. There was a clause in the will which stated that
before the trust can be transferred to my husband, my
marriage must have the approval of the present
trustee."

"WISH ME LUCK, Lewis." The Duke of Winston laid
his monogrammed brush aside and turned to look at
his cousin. "I am about to ask Miss Amelia Allen to
marry me."

Lewis Humphrey choked, spluttered and dabbed at
the drops of spilled wine. He had been comfortably
lounging as he watched the duke complete his toi-
lette. Now he sat up straight and set his wineglass on

the table. "To marry you?" he repeated, as if he had not heard aright.

The duke nodded.

"My dear Guy, I don't know whether it is wise to wish you luck."

"Oh, it will be fortunate if she'll have me," the duke said as he examined himself in the glass.

"*If!* As if any woman in her right mind would refuse you. After all, Guy, you are the Duke of Winston and probably the warmest man in England."

The duke frowned. "I'm not sure that weighs heavily with Amelia. She seems unimpressed by rank and material possessions. As she puts it, she's not of the fashionable world."

"That is another thing, Guy." Lewis stood up, evidently quite agitated. "Do you think she could manage... I mean, as the Duchess of Winston. Your mother would be—"

"I, not my mother, will choose my wife. And Amelia has all the attributes of a perfect lady."

Lewis rubbed his neck. "That may be. But you know what she is."

"Yes, at last I do know. Those days sitting for her have been most revealing." The duke leaned against his dresser and looked at his cousin. "She is a delight, Lewis. So easy to tease and full of humour herself. Delightfully witty and charming. And yet, there's so much strength in her," he said, unable to keep the pride from his voice. "She is probably the youngest person in her father's irregular household. But all of them are dependent upon her, from the old reprobate Timothy to that madcap Melody Harding. And Amelia tries to answer every need. She is so generous, so kindhearted. That is why it was easy for Harry to prey upon her,'' he added bitterly.

Lewis coughed. ''Well, yes. But do think, Guy. A mistress is one thing, but a wife is quite another. Damn it, man, are you willing to take Harry's leavings for your—''

''I shall pretend I did not hear that!'' The duke moved with such menace towards him that Lewis backed away. ''Just understand this. I will marry Amelia Allen if I have to drag her kicking and screaming to the altar. Because I mean to protect her from leeches like Harry. And because I damned well can not live without her!'' He picked up his coat and walked out, leaving a bewildered, gaping Lewis behind.

Ten minutes later, when he was shown into Amelia's drawing room, the duke was sorely disappointed to find Lord Chester with her. Lord Chester, however, appeared pleased to see him.

''Ah, Winston,'' he said, smiling. ''You're just the man I wish to see. Just a formality of course, but I should like your approval. And your felicitations, I hope. Wish me happy, my dear fellow. Miss Allen has just consented to marry me.''

CHAPTER FOURTEEN

"No, Sir, I will not wish you happy! For you certainly shall not marry Miss Allen." His belligerence took Amelia so completely by surprise that she could only stare at him. It was Lord Chester who finally spoke.

"And why not?"

"Because I will not permit it."

"Not permit it?" Chester's surprise, Amelia realized, was as great as her own.

"I am her trustee. Her husband must meet with my approval." The duke hesitated, indeed seemed to flounder. "I ... I cannot in all conscience approve of you."

"My good fellow, are you out of your senses?" Chester still seemed more amazed than irritated. "I am titled, more than moderately wealthy, a substantial, respected—"

"You are a philandering rake! That little nest you maintain at Essex is a veritable landmark. More women have passed through it than bear counting."

"Careful, Winston!" Chester said grimly. "Casting stones, my boy? What is the saying about he who is without sin?"

"It is not my character which is in question."

Amelia bristled. Of course not! *He* was not seeking to marry her. And, like a dog in the manger, he was trying to prevent anyone else from doing so!

"You are abominable!" she exclaimed. "Oh, how can you be so odious!" But her words were lost upon the two men, so enraged had they both become, their heated accusations flying back and forth.

"Blast you!" said Chester. "I'll marry Amelia with or without your permission!"

"The hell you will! The will clearly states—"

"Damn the will! And damn you!"

"So! It little concerns you that Farsdale shall be wrested from her?" the duke accused.

"Oh, the devil with Farsdale! What need have I of another blasted estate!"

Now Amelia's alarmed glance flew to Chester. He had promised! And now he was ready to let Farsdale go, merely in order to have his own way—just as the duke was determined to have his. Both men seemed to have forgotten about her. Well, she certainly would not give up Farsdale and he'd best understand that!

"Henry," she said, trying to gain his attention. "I must say that I—"

"Move aside, my dear." Chester brushed her away. "Let me take charge of this."

The duke also paid her no heed. "You may be willing to give up Farsdale, but let me tell you that I will not allow her to enter penniless into a precarious marriage."

"What the devil do you mean, precarious? She shall be my wife!"

"Never!" the duke thundered.

"Damn it, man, you're not her father. Rave all you choose, but I will marry Amelia."

"Not as I live and breathe!" He moved forward to grasp Chester by the throat.

"Oh, do stop! Please!" Amelia begged as the two men grappled together. "Oh, will you stop this ridiculous brawling?" She rushed forward, trying to separate them, but in vain. Finally Chester was able to break loose. "Not as you live and breathe?" he panted, stepping back and glowering at the duke. "Then so be it!"

"Name your weapon." The duke stood quite still now, but his voice held so much menace that Amelia was terrified.

"Please," she implored. "Neither of you is making sense. You are both overset. If you would but listen to me. I will agree to anything, if only—"

"Pistols," came Chester's even answer. He was not even looking at her.

"No!" she cried, clutching at his sleeve. "You cannot accept his challenge!"

"Hush, my dear," Chester put his arms round her and spoke tenderly. "Have faith! All shall be well."

Idiot! Amelia thought. All shall be well, indeed! After they kill each other? She turned in Chester's arms to appeal to the duke.

"Your grace," she started to say but the pain in his eyes and something else which looked like reproach stunned her into silence.

He transferred his gaze to Chester. "Humphrey will act for me. Have your second contact him." In the next minute he was gone. She tried to stop him, but was held fast by imprisoning arms.

"Do not fret, my dear. You must not overset yourself." Chester clung to her, as if he were trying to reassure himself as well as her. Oblivious to her pleadings, he kept saying, "Hush, my dear. Hush. I must think. There are arrangements to be made."

Soon he, too, was gone and she found herself alone, pacing the floor and wringing her hands, trying to understand what had happened. Why had they both become so incensed?

Chester, she supposed, felt duty-bound to defend her right to marry him.

But the duke? He had looked desperate, and infuriated enough to explode, almost as if she belonged to *him,* and was about to be snatched away. Oh, yes...that was it! He had said it, that awful night at the inn, the night Melody had behaved so outrageously. It had been the first time he had hinted that Amelia might become his mistress. "I have yet to see the contest I cannot match," he had boasted. But this was a game to the death, a game that must be stopped!

Timothy was nowhere to be found, and the carriage was too cumbersome for her to handle. So she hired a hackney. At the duke's quarters she was told by a surprised Driscol that his master was not in, and that he was not aware of his grace's whereabouts, nor was he certain when he would return.

At Chester's house she was met with the same news.

The coachman regarded her with interest as he helped her back into the carriage, and seemed to be awaiting her instructions.

She stared back in silence. Where *did* men go to make these sorts of arrangements? She travelled again to each house, but to no avail. It was almost midnight when she returned to Fitzroy Square.

Melody was abed, but Amelia felt no compunction in arousing and apprising her of the situation. "We must stop them!" she declared when she concluded her story.

"Men!" Melody sat on the edge of her bed, looking strangely plain without her wig and rouge. "They're fools, you know. Always were and always will be."

"Yes," Amelia agreed matter-of-factly. "But I cannot find them. Lord Chester said something about making arrangements and—"

"That's just what they would do." Melody nodded. "Protocol, I think they call it. Setting it up right and proper to murder each other, and over a bit of muslin, mind you! Fools! Why can't they just draw straws or toss a coin or some such?"

Amelia was much too upset to take issue with the reference to herself as a "bit of muslin" or Melody's point of view. "Please, what can we do? How shall we find them?" she pleaded.

"They won't meet until dawn. We have time," said Melody, glancing at the clock. "They always have a surgeon. We'll send Timothy to ferret out the information and then we'll have him follow the doctor."

They found Timothy still up, lolling in his chair, complacently drunk. He smiled at them, blinking. "Come in, ladies. Come in," he said, slurring his words a little. "Fetch some glasses, Melody, and—"

"We ain't drinking and neither are you," Melody said, removing his bottle of rum from the table.

"Oh, Timothy, we need your help," said Amelia.

Timothy blinked and smiled.

"Coffee," said Melody. "We'll need a great deal."

It was not easy. They had to go down into the kitchen, build up the fire and brew the coffee. Still, that was easier than forcing the brew down the protesting Timothy. "Why must I drink this swill when I have perfectly good rum?" he kept demanding as Amelia anxiously glanced through the window, willing away the dawn.

Even when they managed to get him fairly sober, he seemed to have no interest in the fate of either Chester or the duke. It was Melody who finally gained his attention.

"Oh, you numbskull!" she exclaimed. "What about us? If one of them gets killed and the other has to flee the country...either way it will stop the flow of money." Melody gave Amelia a broad wink. Both women knew this was not altogether true, but it served.

"The money?" Timothy blinked at her.

"Think, now—Victor ain't working, the duke has all the say and if he disappears, so will the ready. We'll be out in the street and that leg of yours will rot off, you drunken sot!"

Her practical admonitions soon got through to him. He grabbed his hat and ran out, with Sylvester flapping out after him.

"Oh, catch that bird!" Amelia cried. "He'll spoil everything."

"Oh, never you mind!" Melody said as she sank onto Timothy's bed. "With a bit of luck they'll shoot that blasted bird instead of shooting each other."

THE DUKE, driving his curricle down the Lansbury Road, glanced towards the east. It was a misty morning and the grey dawn was slow in coming. But there would be light enough by the time they arrived at Lansbury Heath. The anger was gone from him now. There was only desperation: a compulsion to put a stop to something which was painful. And puzzling. He had thought she loved Harry Devonshire. Chester's announcement had shocked him out of his senses.

"I say, Guy. It's not too late to call it off." Lewis, on the seat beside him, was still trying to dissuade him. "This is lunacy!"

Amelia had thought so, too. But the sight of her in Chester's arms had drained his mind of logic. Why was she marrying Chester? Had she recognized Harry's diabolical character, or had she merely been playing one man against the other, finally accepting the first who offered marriage?

"This is not like you," Lewis persisted. "You don't even approve of duelling."

No, he didn't, for he had seen enough senseless killing during the War. But never before had he felt that his life...all that meant anything...was being snatched away. He had thought, when he held her in his arms, when she kissed him... Yes, he had thought she loved him. What was even more certain was the fact that, no matter what she was, he loved her, desperately, madly, and he would die before he would let her belong to any other man.

"I will not allow Chester to marry her," he declared through clenched teeth.

"Good Lord, Guy! Be reasonable. If the girl has consented—"

"She doesn't know what she's doing. He's not the right man for her."

"That's not for you to decide. In any case, truth to tell, he may be doing you a favour. Thing is, *she's* not right for— Very well! I'll not say it!" Lewis shook his head. "Next you'll be calling *me* out."

"Not likely, cousin." A ghost of a smile appeared on the duke's face. "I know you mean well. But you don't know Amelia." *Do I?* he wondered sadly. *I only know that I love her.* "Well, we're almost there. Isn't that Chester's carriage under that tree?"

"Hold up, Guy. Do not be so eager." Lewis now sounded quite desperate. "If you can't be reasonable, at least be fair. Damn it, man! It ain't good ton to kill a man just because he's won a woman you fancied."

"The woman I love. And I am not going to kill him. I plan to aim above him." He wondered if he dared to chance wounding him slightly. Just to delay any ceremony, and to give himself a chance to convince Amelia....

"Well, that may not be Chester's plan. And he's a damned good shot. Have you considered that?"

The duke did not answer. He had now pulled in beside Chester's carriage and the other two participants were within earshot. Chester was nervously pacing the ground while his second sat on a stump morosely watching him. Winston jumped lightly down and walked over to join them, and Humphrey reluctantly followed. All nodded a solemn, silent greeting.

Chester had brought his duelling pistols and the two seconds moved aside to examine and load them.

"I been trying to stop this, but I ain't made much progress," confided Lord Morehead, Chester's second. "And you?"

Humphrey shook his head.

Morehead pulled on his ear. "Fact is, I don't exactly know what the quarrel is about. Chester implied that Winston is trying to prevent his marriage."

"That's it."

"Queer. Never took Chester for a marrying man, or a duelling man, neither."

Humphrey brightened. "That's good. Maybe they don't mean to kill each other."

"Hope not," said Morehead. "Let's mark off forty paces to make it more difficult, just in case they do have murder in mind."

"All right," agreed Humphrey. "And while we wait for the surgeon we'll try to— The devil! Here he is."

The surgeon, his black bag in his hand, joined them and took his stand well out of the range of fire. The two seconds paced off the line. The two combatants took their places, pistols in hand, right shoulder to right shoulder.

Humphrey took a deep breath and counted, "Ready! Aim—"

"Heave to, me hearties! Rum!"

The loud squawking which suddenly rent the air startled Chester so that his pistol went off, the bullet whizzing through the trees.

The duke dropped his pistol and wheeled round, lost his balance and fell to his knees as the screeching bird flapped past him.

"Damn!" he exclaimed as he looked up at the man with the wooden leg loping towards him.

"Hoy there, your grace. I would have a word with you," said Timothy.

"You chose a hell of a time to have it," the duke answered, standing up and dusting off his hands. "And what's that mangy parrot doing here?"

"My good man," said Chester, who stalked over. "Do you realize you've just interrupted a—"

"I beg you pardon!" Timothy blinked and his words were a trifle slurred. "But that's just what I come for."

"Then I'm charmed to make your acquaintance, whoever you are!" Humphrey declared, grinning at him.

"Your servant!" Timothy saluted Humphrey, then turned confidentially to the duke. "Wrong man! He ain't the scurvy dog," he said, pointing to Chester.

Chester frowned. "Just what do you mean?"

"No offence, mate." Timothy turned back to the duke. "It's this Devonshire, you see, who's bleeding her dry! He's the scurvy dog who's got her in his clutches and she ain't got nowhere to turn but to you. See?"

"You mean Amelia?" The duke looked at him sharply.

"Exactly. But it ain't her fault. It's that fool of a stepmother of hers. Addlebrained, don't you know. Writing bloody love letters."

The other men were getting rather impatient with this obviously drunken fellow. They started to interrupt him, but the duke waved them off.

"Please continue," he said to Timothy.

"This Devonshire has the bloody letters, you see, and..." In his befuddled state Timothy had gotten his mission to stop the duel confused with getting the letters from Harry Devonshire. He disclosed the whole story to the duke. "I know you're a good 'un. You had that man of yours bring me in out of the rain. I wagered if you knew the facts you might see your way clear to let her have the blunt so she can get rid of the blasted cur."

Winston felt a strong urge to box Amelia's ears, to shake her—and, most of all to take her in his arms and kiss her. But why had she not simply told him the truth!

As for Harry...well, he almost felt he should shake his hand and wish him well. He wasn't her lover, just his old reprehensible, diabolical self, who had finally stooped to blackmail! Well, he'd put a stop to that—at once.

Chester watched the duke leap into his curricle, turn his horses and set them off in a mad gallop down Lansbury Road. Feeling as if a weight had been lifted from him, he mopped the perspiration from his brow and stuck out his chin.

"Well, Morehead, the coward has shown his true colours," he said. "No need to linger here, now that he's run out on us. And I must get to Amelia. She's beside herself with worry.''

Morehead, also greatly relieved, gathered up the duelling pistols, and the two departed in Chester's carriage. The doctor, muttering that there would be no business for him today, also got into his carriage and drove away.

Humphrey did not notice their departure. He had been amused by the sight of the man with the wooden leg shaking his fist at the recalcitrant parrot, which roosted on a tree limb, and utterly fascinated by the salty discourse exchanged between them. It was after the bird was coerced—or perhaps, more properly, *cursed*—back onto the man's shoulder, that Humphrey noticed the three of them were alone.

''My good man,'' he said to Timothy, ''I must say again that I am deeply grateful for your intervention this morning. And I would be most honoured...that is, might I trouble you for a lift into Town in your gig?''

CHAPTER FIFTEEN

AMELIA PACED THE FLOOR. She had little faith in Timothy. She told herself she should have gone with him. If she stood between them, they wouldn't dare shoot! But what good was she doing here? Oh, how she wished it were a nightmare.

But it wasn't a nightmare. It was real. Real pistols and real bullets and one of them probably lying dead by now! Dear God, let it not be him! She thought of the duke, so vital and alive, his hair tousled by the wind, smiling... Oh, he couldn't die. He couldn't. For then she would not wish to live.

They had come down to the front parlour and Melody stayed with her for a while, sitting in the big chair and yawning. Finally she gave it up, saying, "Ain't no use sitting here worrying. We've done all we can do. Best get some rest. It'll soon be morning."

So Amelia sat alone, staring through the window, waiting for the dawn. Frightened of what it would bring.

The long hours passed, as the grey light crept slowly through the mist. Then the mist disappeared and the sun rose higher. Finally she heard the sound of carriage wheels on the cobblestones. She strained to peer out of the window, her heart in her throat.

Oh, no! Chester's carriage!

She ran into the hall and flung the front door wide. Chester bounded up the stairs, his face jubilant.

"All is well, my dear. No impediment remains."

She screamed. "You killed him! Oh, how could you?" She beat upon his chest with both fists. "Oh, how could you kill him!"

"No, no, my sweet. I did not kill him."

He was wounded, then. She must go to him. "Tell me. Where is he? I must go."

"Now, wait, my dear. Calm yourself. He is quite all right." Chester put an arm round her and led her into the parlour while she absorbed his words. Her heart began to beat more evenly.

In the parlour, Chester took both her hands in his and chuckled. "That man of yours gave him the chance to abscond. Just as we got the signal to fire, that fellow Timothy came running down the bank with that bird of his squawking. Went straight to Winston." He released one of her hands to scratch his chin. "Never did get the gist of what he was saying. The man was quite drunk, you know. But Winston ran off like a scared rabbit, and there was no duel."

"Oh, thank God. Oh, I am so glad," she said, and began to laugh, the tears streaming down her face.

"Oh, yes." Chester led her to the settee and sat beside her. "It was rather amusing. I would not have thought Winston could have a yellow streak, but there you have it."

"I'm so glad," she said again, the words catching in her throat. She didn't consider for one moment that the duke was a coward. She wondered what Timothy had said to bring him to his senses. But she didn't care; he was safe, and that was all that mattered. She couldn't seem to stop laughing . . . and crying.

"There, there, my dear." Chester sounded a little alarmed and tried to soothe her. "I know it's been a strain for you. But it's all over now." Gradually she regained her composure and he smiled at her. "That's right, my sweet. You need worry no more. Winston wouldn't dare oppose us now. We can be married immediately."

Married! She stared at him. Yes, she had promised to marry him. And early this morning, because of that promise, he had faced imminent danger. And not once during that whole long night had she thought about him. Her mind, her heart, her whole being had cried out for the duke!

"Henry," she said, haltingly. "I cannot marry you. It would not be fair."

"Not fair?"

"I do not love you. Not in the way you deserve."

"I know, my dear," he said complacently. "You told me that. But I shall be patient. After we are wed—"

"No," she said, gently touching his hand. "You are a kind man. A good and generous man and you deserve a woman whose whole heart will belong to you." *As mine belongs to the duke,* she thought. "You should have more than I can give you."

He started to protest that she was the only woman he wanted.

She touched a finger to his lips. "No, it will not do. I am too fond of you. You must allow me to cry off. One day you will thank me."

To all his protestations she shook her head. At last he went away, saying he would not give up, not until the day she was wed to another.

That will never be, she thought as she made her way wearily upstairs. It would not be fair to marry anyone else, loving the duke as she did. And, she thought, lifting her head, she did not need to enter a loveless match to escape the fate he offered. She was stronger than that!

She would be fully occupied helping to manage her father's household and Farsdale, perhaps doing more painting. Rita had written, requesting more sketches and offering to pay for them! Perhaps others would sit for her... as the duke had.

Then the thought of the duke banished everything else from her mind. It had been so delightful being alone with him in that cosy attic room, she thought as at last she climbed into bed. How they had talked, laughed and teased! She remembered the pleasure she had taken in making those sketches of him, capturing the subtle variations of each fleeting expression. She recalled the way he tightened one corner of his mouth when he was thinking, the quirk of one eyebrow when he teased her, and the slightly sheepish smile that spread across his face when she bested him. She fell asleep, smiling.

She awakened just before noon. She bathed and dressed and went down, feeling a strange sense of anticipation. Would the duke come? Surely he must come eventually, for his portrait; he knew it was finished. She found herself listening for the sound of carriage wheels, and when at last she heard them she rushed to the window.

It was the travelling coach from Farsdale. *Papa!* She ran into the hall and down the front steps to meet him as he alighted from the carriage.

"Oh, Papa!" she cried, embracing him. "How well you look!" He seemed quite his old self, his eyes bright, his face full of colour, as he kissed his daughter, then turned to help his wife down.

"Amelia, dear," Jewel allowed her cheek to touch Amelia's. "Such a wonderful stay we had. You must hear all about it."

She led them into the house. Victor explained that since he felt so much better, he had decided to come back and finish the portraits he had started.

"But then we'll return to Farsdale," Jewel said decisively. "We have met such fine people... very select Society, you know. And it's better there for Victor," she added, almost as an afterthought. "The country air and all."

They refreshed themselves and came down to share the noon meal, at which time Jewel regaled Amelia with accounts of their stay.

"So many parties you would not credit. Everyone wishing to entertain us."

"Parties?" Amelia stared at her. She had not met one single neighbour during her stay at Farsdale.

"Yes, but don't be alarmed, my dear." Jewel held up her fork. "During the first two weeks we were there

I received all the callers myself. I made it perfectly clear that his lordship was resting."

Amelia swallowed, choked and put down her fork. "His lordship?"

"Of course. You do remember that your father is the Marquis de Beauchante, don't you? I let that be known as soon as we arrived. You know how servants gossip." She toyed with her fish. "And I was right. It set the proper tone. Everyone was vying for the favour of Lord and Lady Beauchante."

Amelia looked at her father, wondering how he felt about all this. He had never cared about rank or title. But, she thought, he always enjoyed good company. He had been glancing through his accumulated mail, seemingly oblivious to Jewel's chatter. As if he felt her gaze, he looked across at her.

"Amy, dear, I've been wondering. The dower house at Farsdale is standing empty. But it has excellent light. Would you mind if I set up a studio there?"

She said, of course, that it would be a good idea and the talk reverted to how the house should be remodelled and what would be needed. Amelia breathed a sigh of thanks. It appeared that both Jewel and Victor would be happy at Farsdale.

After lunch, Victor retired to his room and Jewel followed Amelia into the small sitting room.

"The letters, Amelia," she said anxiously. "Did you get them from Harry?"

"I . . . well, not exactly. That is, not yet."

"Not yet? It's been several weeks. Oh, my dear, it would be dreadful, you know, to be so exposed after we have established ourselves so well. You promised. What on earth have you been doing?''

Amelia stirred with vexation. After all, it was Jewel's own fault that they were all in such a coil. And if Jewel only knew what she had been through! Still, she had promised. Then so much had happened, she had forgotten all about the letters.

"You need not be concerned," she said. "I shall have them soon." As soon as the duke paid her for the portrait, she thought, she and Melody and Timothy would call on Harry.

WHEN THE DUKE called on Harry, he was not at home. After spending most of the day fruitlessly trying to track him down, he returned to Harry's quarters and awaited him there. When the culprit returned about midnight, it did not take the duke long to give him the thrashing he deserved and wrest the letters from him.

"That is all. Only three," Harry declared, nursing his swollen jaw. "Upon my honour!"

"I know how little your honour signifies," scoffed the duke. "But understand this! If ever you go near Miss Amelia Allen again, or threaten her in any way, you shall answer to me!"

The duke, unlike Amelia, had made no promise to Jewel. So when he reached his own quarters, he felt no compunction in perusing the provocative outpouring contained in her letters. He shook his head in utter disbelief. Addlebrained! The fellow with the wooden leg had been right.

The duel! Thoughts of the fellow and his parrot brought it all back. Damn! What had Chester, all of them, thought when he'd rushed off? Chester was probably prattling even now about that coward, the Duke of Winston! *Well, so be it,* he thought, chuckling as he climbed into bed.

He hadn't had any desire to kill Chester, or even wound him, he thought sleepily. *Nice enough fellow. Just didn't want him to marry Amelia.*

He sat up, paralyzed by a sudden thought. He was a fool! He had spent the whole day, and half the night, chasing Harry Devonshire, leaving the field clear for Chester. Even now, the pair could be on their way to Gretna Green!

He leapt out of bed, pulled the bell rope for Driscol, and scrambled into his clothes. He would pursue them—to the ends of the earth if necessary. If he were too late, if they were already married... by gad, he might have to kill Chester after all.

"Your grace?" Driscol, in nightclothes, blinked sleepily at him.

"Get into your riding clothes. We have an errand."

They went on horseback directly to Chester's house. The duke waited anxiously while Driscol retreated to the stable to arouse Chester's groom.

"Lord Chester has been abed since ten," he reported after a few minutes. "And there are no travelling plans for tomorrow. In fact—"

"Never mind," said the duke, greatly relieved. Still, he could take no chances. He instructed Driscol to post himself outside Chester's house for the rest of the night.

"If you see any movement, any indication at all of preparations for a long trip, come for me immediately." There was nothing more he could do at present. Wearily, he returned home and fell into a restless sleep.

IT WAS AFTER NINE when Driscol returned the next morning to report that Lord Chester had departed with two of his cronies at an early hour.

"Blockhead!" exclaimed the duke. "I told you to come for me if—"

"But their destination was Lord Morehead's estate in Yorkshire, your grace. And they went in Morehead's carriage."

"Gone to the country," the duke said dubiously. "Are you sure?"

"Just so, your grace. I followed them for a piece just to make sure." Driscol's mouth twisted in a knowing smile before he added, "Quite the opposite direction from a certain Fitzroy Square residence."

"Well, wipe that blasted grin off your face and fetch my shaving gear!" the duke growled. But inwardly, he was jubilant. Chester was an even bigger fool than he. To go on a country jaunt with such a prize as Amelia Allen in the offing! He was probably planning a big wedding ceremony to introduce his beautiful bride to the ton, feeling secure in the knowledge that the cowardly Duke of Winston had withdrawn from the fray. Or, as Chester was most certainly putting it, "had run from the field in terror for his life!"

Well, my friend, you have a good deal to learn, the duke thought, as he took up his shaving brush with confidence and determination. He swished the shaving brush round and round in the soap bowl, then paused. Amelia was not just any woman. And she was not to be won by the usual enticements. Slowly he lathered his face. Could she really love Chester? Impossible! He was not the right man for her and he must make her understand that. If only he could spend enough time with her to let her know how much he loved her, how happy he could make her. She was not entirely indifferent to him, he was sure. There had been times when he was sitting for her that he had felt she liked . . . more than liked him. That was it! He'd commission another portrait! Damn it, he'd commission a dozen portraits, if necessary.

And as for the portrait she had already done, that would be his excuse for calling this morning. He would like it and would pay the price she had asked. She would be so relieved, thinking how she would be able to deal with Harry. Then he would give her the letters and tell her she need never fear that rascal again. He smiled as he pulled on his jacket. He couldn't wait to see her face—and the grateful look that would surely be on it. Surely then she'd recognize his finer qualities and her heart would be touched.

This time, when he arrived at Fitzroy Square, the door was opened by a tall grey-haired man, a man who seemed to have all the professional courtesy of a proper butler as he took his card and said, "I'll see if Miss Allen is in, your grace. Will you wait in the parlour with her ladyship?"

He followed the fellow, wondering who the devil was "her ladyship." His eyes opened wide at the sight of the beautiful woman who rose to greet him. She was a vision in a pale blue morning dress that matched her eyes, bright golden tresses piled high on her head, and a dazzling smile. He had seen her once before. Where?

"Your grace, how delightful to see you again." Even her voice was provocative.

"And a pleasure to see you, my lady." He tried to recall... this woman had once tiptoed up to whisper in his ear...of course! At that rout where Amelia had suddenly appeared and knocked over all those glasses.

"Did you come to see Victor? He is resting. We just arrived from Farsdale yesterday. A rather tiring trip, you know."

Farsdale! So this was the stepmother.

"Perhaps I can be of assistance, your grace? Did you wish to arrange for a sitting? I am not certain how long we shall remain in London, but..."

He looked at her, not listening. She was the reason for Amelia's clumsy interruption that evening, which had been a deliberate attempt to stop her stepmother's blatant flirting, to protect the father she adored from embarrassment or hurt. Yes, and this was the foolish female who had penned those ridiculous lines to Harry.

Suddenly he was furious with this woman, who had behaved like a lightskirt and left Amelia to deal with her folly! He thought of Amelia being bullied by Harry, of her expedition to a tavern of ill repute, where she had been subjected to all manner of insults—all because of this wicked woman standing before him. He was forced to call upon all the restraints imposed by his noble birth and bearing to keep from smiting her. Instead, he struck in the only way he could.

"I believe you have some interest in these," he said, taking the letters from his pocket.

Her face went deathly pale. "Where did you get those?"

"Harry—"

"Oh, Amelia gave me her word there would be no scandal, and now just look what the vexatious creature has done. To involve a duke in my affair. She will not get away with this. I shall call her immediately."

"You will not disturb Amelia. It was for her sake that I retrieved these letters."

"Oh. Oh, your grace, how silly of me, of course. So kind of you." Now her face was wreathed with smiles. "I have been so worried. And I am deeply grateful," she said, holding out her hand. "I shall destroy them immediately."

He shook his head. "I think not." She must make no more trouble for Amelia. He returned the letters to his pocket. "I'll keep these as insurance."

"Insurance?"

"That you will remain a dutiful and faithful wife," he said. "Fear of their disclosure may cause you to refrain from any indiscreet amorous impulses."

Jewel drew herself up in genuine amazement. "That was just a youthful folly," she said, gesturing towards the letters in his pocket. "Surely, your grace, you must know that I would not now behave in such an unseemly manner. I am now Lady Beauchante of Farsdale."

He was still trying to decide how to answer this when the man who had opened the door returned to inform him that, "Miss Allen awaits you in the studio, your grace."

He mounted the stairs slowly, feeling a great deal of apprehension. Would she be angry with him for starting the quarrel with Chester? Or defiant, determined to go forth with her marriage plans?

She ran to him as soon as he entered the attic, clasped his hands in hers and gazed up at him with shining eyes. "Oh, I am so relieved you came to your senses. I was desperately afraid that you would not. I am so glad that you . . . that both of you are safe."

He looked down at her, basking in the warm glow of her eyes, holding tightly to her hand.

"Oh, dear," she said, suddenly looking a little embarrassed and pulling away from him. "I mustn't get paint on you." He saw that she was holding a wet paintbrush in one hand. Her hair was dishevelled, there was a paint smudge on one cheek and she was enveloped in that voluminous smock she always wore when she was painting. And she had never looked more desirable.

"I was doing another sketch for Rita," she explained, moving over to put down her brush and wipe her hands on a rag smelling of turpentine. "Oh, my lord. You cannot imagine my relief. I am so grateful no harm came to Lord Chester. He has always been one of my family's staunchest friends."

Chester! He stiffened. Was it too late? Had he lost to Chester?

Now she moved to the easel that held his portrait. "Please stand over here," she said. "I wish you to see it in the best light." He moved as she directed, and she slowly pulled away the cover to reveal his likeness. She watched him anxiously. "Do you like it?"

He looked at the painting, seeing himself as he never had before. He was sitting with his legs crossed, holding a riding crop in one hand. But it was as if life had been breathed into the canvas. The colour, vitality and force of everything he felt was reflected there: the uninhibited joy of cavorting with a redheaded girl through an overgrown field as they chased a brightly coloured bird, the laughter and the dismay when she limped away from him, one shoe off and one shoe on. There, too, was wind and sunshine and the exhilaration of galloping beside her across meadows full of the fresh scent of wet grass and the gurgle of a brook.

This was a living portrait of a man who was in love—and who was loved in return? Surely *her* love was also reflected there.

He turned to her. "You do love me!"

She nodded, as if in resignation.

"You cannot marry Chester!"

"No. He deserves more than I can give him. I told him so yesterday."

Relief and joy swept through him. He gathered her in his arms, ran a hand through her tangled curls, smothered her smudged face with kisses, breathing in the scent of paint and turpentine. "Oh, my darling, my sweet. I shall make you so happy, just as I promised. I shall always love you."

Perhaps not always, she thought as she tightened her arms round his neck. Mistresses are so casually tossed away. But the thought was erased as his lips touched hers and ecstasy spiralled through her. She felt herself come alive, full of the joy, the passion, the love she could never find with anyone else.

"Forgive me," she silently cried to the memory of her mother, "but I'd rather spend one day with him than a dozen years as a proper wife to another man. I love him as you loved Papa." Somehow she knew Venetia would understand.

He lifted her in his arms, sat on Timothy's bench and cradled her in his lap. "We must make plans, my love."

"Plans?" She snuggled against his chest. Where should they go first? Perhaps a tour of the Continent, she thought, travelling alone. She sat up to tell him so, "First, your grace—"

He placed a finger on her lips. "My name is Guy. Guy Grosvenor."

She stared at him, then gave a gurgle of laughter. Oh, she was a wanton! Abandoning herself utterly to a man whose name she did not know. "Guy," she said. "It will do nicely. As I recall, you mentioned something about touring the Greek isles. Would tomorrow be too soon?"

He brushed a curl from her forehead. "I should think so, my love. First, I must get a licence, and speak to your Papa. He might want a big wedding. And truth to tell, I'd rather like to show you off to everyone before setting sail."

"Wedding?" She sat up again and pushed away from him. "Do you mean you want to marry me?"

"Of course I want to marry you. What did you think?"

"What *was* I to think?" she exclaimed, wondering why she felt so cross. "All these months you have given every indication that you wished nothing more from me than to be your mistress. I expected a proposition, not a proposal!"

"And you were ready to go off with me willy-nilly, asking and demanding nothing!" He stood up, releasing her abruptly. He gripped her shoulders and glared at her. "You are an unconventional piece of baggage, Amelia Allen! That heart of yours will always be getting you into scrapes. When you are my wife, I mean to protect you from—" He broke off as she began to laugh.

She couldn't help it. She laughed and laughed. They were quarrelling because he wanted to marry her! And more than anything in the world she wanted to be his wife. "I'm not unconventional," she sputtered. "I wouldn't be anyone else's mistress—only yours. Because I love you."

"I know," he said, handing her his handkerchief. "As I love you. As I did, even before I understood your true worth. I had come to ask you to marry me when Chester announced your betrothal to him. I was never so furious and frightened at the thought of losing you." He shrugged. "Now you know why I challenged him."

She looked at him with wonder. "Even then you wanted to marry me?"

"Even then, and even though I thought you loved Harry."

"*Harry?* I must tell you the truth."

He smiled. "No need. Your friend Timothy disclosed the whole story. That is why I abandoned the duel." He held up the letters.

"Oh, you got them! Oh, thank you, Guy," she said, throwing her arms about him. "Jewel will be so relieved. I must go and tell her.

"No," he said. "I have already dealt with Jewel. Just as I mean to deal with anything or anyone who dares trouble you. Oh, my love," he said, holding her close. "I know you are a determined and willful lady, but please do not ever keep secrets from me again. Always let me love and protect you."

"Yes. Just as I shall always love and protect you," she whispered and his lips descended upon hers, tender, possessive, urging. And she was all his—warm and weak and yielding.

EPILOGUE

READERS of the London *Gazette,* of June 18, 1820, encountered the following notice of interest:

During the month of July, a display of the exquisite scrimshaws of Mr. Timothy Randall will be on view at 41 Fitzroy Square. Mr. Randall, a talented artisan, is considered somewhat eccentric and is often seen with a parrot perched upon his shoulder. His history remains elusive, but rumour has it that he is a former naval officer whose heroic activities cost him a leg at Trafalgar. However, Miss Rita LaCrosse, well known for her renditions of comic opera, and a friend of Mr. Randall contends he is a Spanish nobleman who fled that country after a duel in which his assailant was slain. Whatever his true identity may be, Mr. Randall's scrimshaws are exceptional. Persons wishing to purchase pieces of these choice works should contact Madam Melody Harding at Randall's studio in Fitzroy Square.

This establishment was once the residence and studio of the well-known portrait painter Mr. Victor Allen. Mr. Allen, who is also the Marquis de Beauchante of France, now resides with his charming wife at his country estate, Farsdale, near Covington Corners, Sussex, where he consents to execute the occasional portrait for a very select group of sitters. The marquis is also said to enjoy the country air and the frequent visits of his grandchildren and their parents, Their Graces the Duke and Duchess of Winston.

Coming in March from

LaVyrle Spencer's unforgettable story of a
love that wouldn't die.

LAVYRLE SPENCER

SWEET MEMORIES

She was as innocent as she was unsure . . . until a very special
man dared to unleash the butterfly wrapped in her cocoon and
open Teresa's eyes and heart to love.

SWEET MEMORIES is a love story to savor that will make you
laugh—and cry—as it brings warmth and magic into your
heart.

''Spencer's characters take on the richness of friends, relatives
and acquaintances.''
—*Rocky Mountain News*

SWEET

RELIVE THE MEMORIES....

All the way from turn-of-the-century Ellis Island to the future of the '90s...A CENTURY OF AMERICAN ROMANCE takes you on a nostalgic journey through the twentieth century.

Watch for all the A CENTURY OF AMERICAN ROMANCE titles coming to you one per month over the next two months in Harlequin American Romance, including #385 MY ONLY ONE by Eileen Nauman, in April.

Don't miss a day of A CENTURY OF AMERICAN ROMANCE.

The women...the men...the passions...the memories....

If you missed #345 AMERICAN PIE, #349 SATURDAY'S CHILD, #353 THE GOLDEN RAIN-TREE, #357 THE SENSATION, #361 ANGELS WINGS, #365 SENTIMENTAL JOURNEY, #369 STRANGER IN PARADISE, #373 HEARTS AT RISK, or #377 TILL THE END OF TIME and would like to order them, send your name, address, and zip or postal code, along with a check or money order for $2.95 plus 75¢ postage and handling ($1.00 in Canada) *for each book ordered,* payable to Harlequin Reader Service, to.

In the U.S.
3010 Walden Ave.
Box 1325
Buffalo, NY 14269-1325

In Canada
P.O. Box 609
Fort Erie, Ontario
L2A 5X3

Please specify book title(s) with your order.
Canadian residents please add applicable federal and provincial taxes.

CA-80

Everyone loves a spring wedding, and this April,
Harlequin cordially invites you to read the most
romantic wedding book of the year.

With This Ring

**ONE WEDDING—FOUR LOVE STORIES
FROM OUR MOST DISTINGUISHED
HARLEQUIN AUTHORS:**

BETHANY CAMPBELL
BARBARA DELINSKY
BOBBY HUTCHINSON
ANN McALLISTER

*The church is booked, the reception arranged and the
invitations mailed. All Diane Bauer and Nick Granatelli
have to do is walk down the aisle. Little do they realize that
the most cherished day of their lives will spark so many
romantic notions....*

Available wherever Harlequin books are sold.

COMING IN 1991 FROM
HARLEQUIN SUPERROMANCE:

THE·BYRNSIDE·INHERITANCE

1

Three abandoned orphans,
one missing heiress!

Dying millionaire Owen Byrnside receives an
anonymous letter informing him that twenty-six years
ago, his son, Christopher, fathered a daughter. The
infant was abandoned at a foundling home that
subsequently burned to the ground, destroying all
records. Three young women could be Owen's long-
lost granddaughter, and Owen is determined to track
down each of them! Read their stories in

#434 HIGH STAKES (available January 1991)
#438 DARK WATERS (available February 1991)
#442 BRIGHT SECRETS (available March 1991)

Three exciting stories of intrigue and romance by
veteran Superromance author Jane Silverwood.

words a little." "Fetch some glasses, Melody, and—